THE ADVENTURES OF HYPERKID

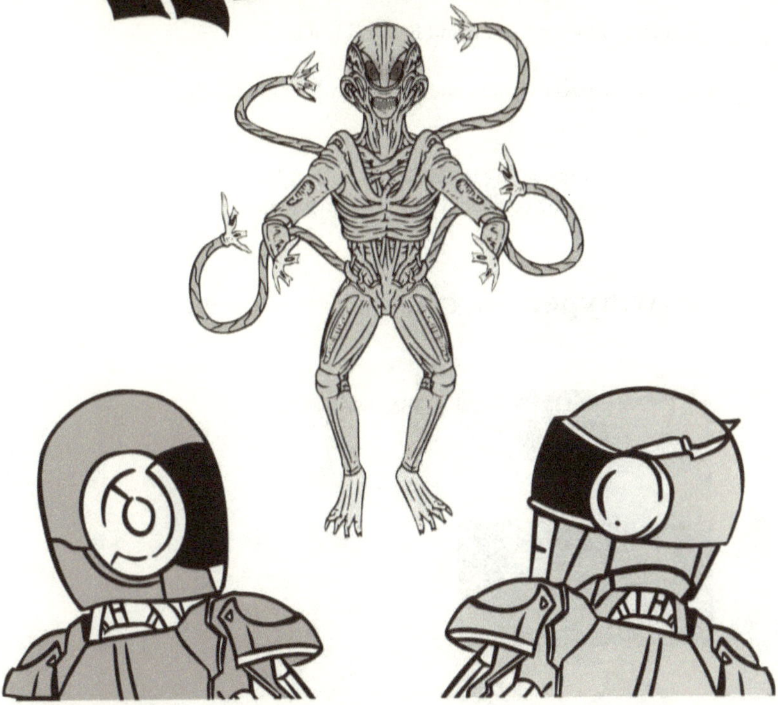

BOOK 2

THE CYBORG AT THE END OF THE UNIVERSE

BY EMERSON DAUB AND RICHARD DAUB

www.hyperkid.xyz

ISBN: 978-1-946094-00-1

To all intelligent life beyond Earth:

*Despite what you may have heard about our
planet, we come in peace.*

THE CYBORG AT THE END OF THE UNIVERSE

CHAPTER 1

It isn't easy being a famous super hero. In fact, sometimes it doesn't really seem fair. Here you are helping citizens in need and saving the planet and signing autographs and taking selfies with people and so on, yet you still have to go to school and do your homework and clean your room and do whatever else your parents tell you to do. This leaves little time for playing video games and constructing robotic creatures with Blockos, those little plastic building blocks that are made in one of those Scandinavian countries that Daddy is always bragging that some of his Viking ancestors came from.

My name is Morgan Wallace, and I am also the super hero known as HyperKid. My best friend Brian Bullini is the super hero known as BullBorg. We both acquired cyborg super powers after being exposed to the radioactive rays of a meteor shower during the summer before fourth grade. My cat Ralston was also exposed to the rays and is now a cyborg cat, but he's not a super hero.

Brian and I may be best friends now, but it didn't start out that way. When he first moved to West Plains from our rival neighbor town East Plains at the beginning of fourth grade, people thought that he was a bully. He was bigger than the rest of us, and he was wearing ripped jeans and a flannel shirt with the sleeves ripped off and a t-shirt with a bull skull

on it. He grunted at us when our teacher Mrs. Crabcake introduced us to him, and then later that day he started scaring the other kids away on the playground by roaring at them. His first day only seemed to confirm what all of us kids at West Plains Elementary had been hearing since kindergarten: *Kids from East Plains are evil monsters.*

Even before he started scaring kids on the playground, I immediately thought that he was my arch enemy. I thought that all super heroes had to have arch enemies, and when he walked into the classroom on that first day of fourth grade, my cyborg sensors said that he was also known as "Bull the Bully" and that I should "BEWARE". The sensors also said that he was a red meteor type, so I just figured that meant he was a villain because my meteor type was green. Later that same day is when he started scaring away all the other kids on the playground. As the new super hero HyperKid, I thought it was my duty to defend the other kids and take back the playground. After encountering HyperKid for the first time, Brian then created his own super hero identity BullBorg. He thought I was the villain who was attacking him and violating his personal space, and he saw himself as a super hero who had to defeat the villainous HyperKid.

But it was all a giant misunderstanding. It didn't take me long to realize that he wasn't really a bully at all. Bullies usually find the weakest targets and start tormenting them, but Brian wasn't like that. He was just trying to scare everyone away because he was actually afraid of *us*. He had always heard that West Plains kids were evil monsters (which seemed ridiculous since West Plains is ranked the 57th greatest small-to-midsize medium city in the United States), and he felt like he was alone in enemy territory. Brian was also very self-conscious about his appearance because he knew he looked different than the other kids, and sometimes kids are mean when they encounter someone who looks different, especially when it's a new kid. He just assumed the other kids were going to make fun of him, so he figured that being scary would prevent the other kids from picking on him. But it only made it worse.

Brian is also hyperactive like me. Being hyperactive sometimes makes you feel different than the other kids. Sometimes I worry that something is wrong with me and I just want to hide from the rest of the world. I think Brian felt the same way. Hyperactive kids also sometimes have trouble controlling their emotions, so he acted out whenever it felt like the outside world was moving too fast and being too loud. It's hard to stay calm when it feels like this, and sometimes you feel like screaming to make the noise stop. I definitely know that feeling.

But soon I started to understand how he felt. I also started to realize that I was probably the only kid who could understand how he felt because the rest of the kids didn't seem to understand how I felt. He started to seem less like an arch enemy and more like someone who could be a friend. And this was not only because we were hyperactive, but also because having cyborg super powers makes us *very* different than everyone else. He seemed like the only person in the world who would truly understand who I was, and I was probably the only person who could understand who he truly was.

So, like I said, it was all a just misunderstanding. He was scared of us, and we were scared of him. We were all wrong because we hadn't given each other a chance to get to know each other and instead made judgments about each other based on rumors and assumptions. Even my cyborg system had failed because it said that Brian was also known as "Bull the Bully", but that's actually just what Brian named the bull skull on his shirt. He just thinks bulls and skulls are fashionably cool. Daddy says that this is just another example of fake news causing real world problems.

Anyway, we would all soon find out what a true hero Brian was when he and I saved our classmates after our teacher Mrs. Crabcake farted and set the classroom on fire. As HyperKid and BullBorg in our special fire armor, we got the kids out of there and put the fire out and kept the whole school from

burning down. Our identities were no longer a secret, but that's okay because nobody got hurt. This event cemented our friendship, and after that we became the most famous super heroes in West Plains and formed the West Plains Super Hero League. Brian actually became more popular than me because the other kids now saw him as the cool rebel, while I was the quiet one with the glasses. But that's okay because I'm not a big fan of the glaring spotlight, and my dream of becoming a famous cyborg super hero had actually come true.

But as I was saying earlier, being a famous super hero isn't all it's cracked up to be. It has its perks, but there's a lot of boring stuff that comes along with it that takes away from your time to have fun doing stuff that you like to do. My least favorite thing about it was working for Mayor Maria Martinez, who gave us giant keys to the city after the fire (I'm still *extremely*

disappointed that these keys don't actually work—I was hoping mine would be the key to a castle or a high-tech hover carrier).

During the giant key ceremony, Mayor Martinez asked us to come work for her to protect the citizens of West Plains from injustice. That sounded great at first, but all we ever did when we showed up for work was take pictures with her and her politician friends. What was most annoying was that they all thought we looked "so cute" in our costumes. None of them took us seriously, and not once were we ever actually asked to do anything to actually help the citizens of West Plains. It seemed like the only thing these politicians were interested in was making themselves look good by showing up and having their pictures taken with the people who were actually doing the real work like the firefighters, police officers, emergency services, volunteers, school teachers, local business owners, and so on. Besides taking pictures, the only other thing they ever seemed to do was raise money to support their election campaigns. But they never tried to raise money to help people who actually needed it.

Brian eventually quit working for Mayor Martinez because he said that she was using the West Plains Super Hero League to promote her ideologically flawed political agenda. It was strange to hear Brian talk like this, but it was around this time when Brian stopped trying to hide his true intelligence.

"These politicians aren't working for us," he said. "They are only trying to advance their own political careers. They don't care at all about you or me or anyone else. I can't stand by and allow this to happen. I am going to do something about this."

To everyone's surprise, Brian turned out to be a genius. I think being around these sleazy politicians and realizing how much smarter he was than they were made something inside of him wake up. He started reading all the time, even during recess, and by the end of fourth grade he was smarter than most of the teachers. I began to wonder if he had some kind of genius super power that I didn't have, but he said that super powers had nothing to do with it.

After Brian quit working for Mayor Martinez, I wanted to quit too. When I asked Mommy and Daddy if I could, I was expecting them to say things like how it was a good experience for me and how I should stick with it, but to my surprise they both agreed to it without me having to convince them. They said that they too were frustrated by the behavior of our elected officials, and they were also worried that I was doing too much with this super hero stuff. They said it was important to have some down time when I could relax and just be my regular plain self.

After I quit working for Mayor Martinez, Daddy and I started working on a writing project together that told the story of everything that happened since I acquired my cyborg powers. Normally I don't like writing, but Daddy is a writer and this was a different kind of writing than what I usually had to do in school. So I sat down with him every day for a couple of weeks and told him everything that happened, and he wrote it all down and asked me lots of questions until his whole notebook was filled up. He then typed up his notes on the computer and turned them into what he called a "first person narrative", which is basically me telling the story like I am doing now. Then he had me read this narrative and I told him what needed to be changed and added some other stuff that I had forgotten about. I also suggested that he shorten some of his character's lectures that he gave my character in the book because they were way too long and that kids who are reading it might get bored, so he said he would take it under editorial advisement. But then he left them all in anyway and even made some of them longer. Even so, I still think it came out pretty good, and he was right about this being a fun kind of writing. So, after all the editing was done and the grammar mistakes were corrected, Daddy then uploaded the file to some website and a few days later a package showed up in the mail with the finished version of *The Adventures of HyperKid, Volume 1: HyperKid v BullBorg*. That was really cool!

My teachers and the kids at school were amazed that me and Daddy had written a real book. I thought Brian would love the book too, but he wrote a very critical review of it that appeared in the local paper that called the writing style "not even worthy of the sensationalistic tabloid rags that litter the newsstands of our great nation". He did like the part where BullBorg and HyperKid saved the kids from the fire, but that was pretty much it.

Brian was acting weirder and weirder every day, and towards the end of the year he did start to become less popular because his head was always buried in a book and he started ignoring people. Mommy and Daddy said that sometimes hyperactive people lock on to something and become so extremely focused on it that they block out everything else. I think this was starting to happen to Brian with his studies.

But even though Brian wrote a bad review, the book was still a huge success. Daddy and I were interviewed by newspaper reporters, radio hosts, television hosts, podcast hosts, bloggers, and so on, and HyperKid became a social media sensation. It was fun at first, but after a while it became a dull routine, and then it just became annoying. Fortunately Daddy said we could take a break from promoting the book to start working on material for the next one. But this was even more annoying because he started following me around the house with his notebook and asking me questions about what happened at school and if I did anything heroic that day. It got to the point where I always said nothing happened even if something actually did. I just wanted to have a little Morgan time without HyperKid. When he realized that he wasn't getting good material from me, he started following my little brother Parker around when he noticed that he might have super powers. Parker is five now, and I don't think he actually does have super powers, but he is really good at playing video games—and not just the ones that are for little kids that help you learn stuff like math and spelling. He is good at *my* big kid video games. He started playing more than me and actually got better than I am at some of them, including the *Blockos Galactic Super Hero League Ultimate Building Blocks Omniverse* game. Now Parker hardly ever touches his toys anymore. Daddy thinks that being good at video games is Parker's super power. While I don't really agree with that, I didn't say anything to Daddy so that he would keep following Parker around instead of me.

As for my old cat Ralston, he actually does have cyborg super powers too because he was sleeping on my bed during the meteor shower last summer, but he doesn't use them much. Daddy says Ralston's only powers are his abilities to take twelve hour naps and to puke on the rug after eating the packing tape on boxes we get in the mail. But I have seen him point his laser eye out the window to scare away the alley cats and squirrels in our yard, so he does use them sometimes. The cats stopped coming around, but the squirrels managed to make a hole on our roof and break into the attic. When Daddy went out to the store to buy a squirrel trap, Ralston somehow managed to trap them in my old toy castle and then patch up the hole in the roof by stuffing a blanket in it with his cyber paw. Mommy was impressed with Ralston, but Daddy said it was nothing special and started mumbling to himself about how it doesn't make sense that Ralston can't use his powers to clean his litter box, but as soon as he catches a couple of squirrels and patch the roof, suddenly he's Mr. Super Hero Cat. Mommy says Daddy is still a bit disappointed that he wasn't able to train Ralston to do stuff around the house like empty the dishwasher and mow the lawn and take out the garbage, but that he'll get over it. Eventually.

Anyway, fourth grade was the most amazing year of my life, but I was glad when the last day of school came in June. When school started again in the fall, Parker would be starting kindergarten and we would be going to the same school for the first time. But I didn't want to think about school at all. I just wanted to enjoy the summer. I would be turning ten in July, and Parker would now be old enough to go to the same summer camp as me. While summer camp at the WPYC (West Plains Youth Center) wasn't my favorite thing in the world, it's still better than going to school, especially since there's no homework. And even though Parker and I would be in different groups, it would be fun having him there. Mommy and Daddy also planned our usual upstate vacation at the Sparkling Timber Lake Resort and Mountain Spa, which was always fun because they had a heated pool and Wi-Fi.

Although it looked like it was going to be a great summer, I couldn't stop thinking about Alien-Bot emerging from the wormhole in the sky during our ceremony with Mayor Martinez last year. Alien-Bot is an Alien Robot Cyborg (also known as an "ARC") and classified as a villain who is wanted in 23 different galaxies for hacking, trespassing, and threatening to destroy the universe. I don't know exactly why he showed up here, but it surely has something to do with Brian and I because he scanned only us and ignored the rest of the crowd before going back into the wormhole and disappearing.

It all had to be connected somehow. Alien-Bot must have had something to do with us turning into cyborgs, and I didn't think it was just a coincidence that Brian and I were the

only two kids in the greater West Plains metropolitan area who were transformed into cyborgs with super powers. Brian and I hadn't even met each other yet when the meteor shower happened, so I thought maybe our hyperactivity had something to do with it. But since we both turned out to be heroes and not villains, we still had no idea why Brian's meteor type was red and mine was green. My super hero sense was telling me that it had to mean something... but what?

My super hero sense also told me that Alien-Bot would be back. That feeling kept getting stronger as the dog days of summer wound down and the first day of fifth grade got closer. I knew that we both had to be ready when he did finally return, and that meant making a visit to Sven's Garage for some upgrades.

CHAPTER 2

When I first became a cyborg last year, Mommy brought me to our family physician Dr. Popsicle to see if he could help turn me back into a regular kid. Doc Pop wasn't able to help, but he mentioned a mechanic named Sven who owned a garage down the street from his office. He said that Sven worked on all sorts of stuff from import cars to motorcycles to vacuum cleaners and even some top secret stuff.

It sounded too crazy to Mommy and Daddy to take a kid to a mechanic to get fixed, but since there was no other immediate solution, I was able to talk them into letting me stay a cyborg and to use my new powers as a super hero. The next day I received a mask from the Shanghai SuperTech Corp that covered up my visible cyborg parts so that I could look like my normal self when I'm not HyperKid, and Mommy and Daddy set up some rules that I had to follow such as not hurting anyone, calling 911 if there was a serious emergency situation, and making sure my homework was done before I did any super hero stuff. Later we received message saying that if something goes wrong with my software or hardware, I should go to Sven's Garage for repairs.

I hadn't met Sven yet, so I didn't really know anything about him or if he even did upgrades. But taking on Alien-Bot seemed like a much bigger task than defending the playground from bullies or putting out classroom fires, and he seemed like the only one who could possibly help. At the time my only defensive weapon was my laser shooter that could stun enemies but not hurt them, and that didn't seem like enough to stop someone who wanted to destroy the universe. So, over the summer I spent a lot of time thinking about what upgrades I was going to need, and one day I went up to my room and made a drawing that I could give to Sven:

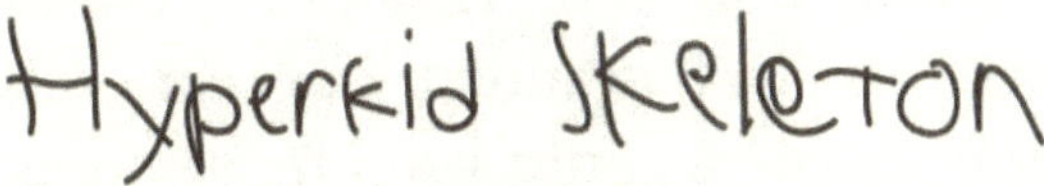

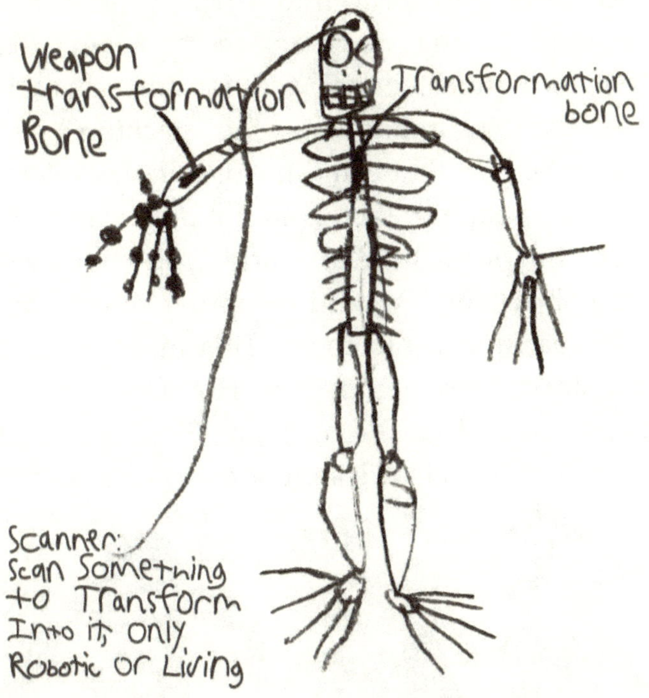

I drew a skeleton because the upgrades had to be implanted inside my body. I tried to keep it simple, so I designed only three tech pieces.

The first two pieces worked together: a visual scanner in my forehead that could scan any biological or mechanical/robotic object, and a "transformation bone" that the scanner feeds into that can transform you into that object. So, if I scanned our cat Ralston or Mommy's car, I could keep those scans on file and then transform into them at any time without having to scan them again. The transformation bone is located in the breastbone (also known as the "sternum"), and that's the part that can transform your skeleton into any shape or size. And not only could you scan things in the real world, you could also scan objects on TVs and computer screens and then transform into them. This meant I could transform into heroes like Hot Dog Guy or Green Bean Man or a villain like Trash Can Man. I could also design some cool armor in

my video games and scan those, and I could even transform into BullBorg if I wanted to!

Then there would be a "weapon transformation bone" implanted into my cyborg arm that could be transformed into a large cannon blaster and shoot fire, ice, lava, slime, high-powered lasers, fire extinguishing foam, or whatever else the situation called for. It would also have a healing function that could heal my own injuries or someone else's. I also wanted to ask Sven to hack my fire armor so that I could deploy it whenever I wanted. The fire armor currently had some kind of lock on it and could only deploy when my cyborg system determined that there was a fire-related emergency.

I thought the drawing was some of my best work ever, but I was a little worried about showing it to Mommy and Daddy because they probably wouldn't like the weapon upgrades. But Brian and I both needed these upgrades if we were going to face Alien-Bot, which would not be our decision. Bad guys usually went after super heroes first, and he already seemed to know about us. We had to be ready or else we might be annihilated.

Daddy would be easier to convince than Mommy because he liked super heroes when he was a kid and is actually still into all that stuff. But Mommy would be worried about the weapons being illegal because she's a lawyer (the good kind of lawyer who tries to help

people, not one of those lawyers who chases ambulances or tries to get people with boo-boos to file million dollar lawsuits). She had to understand that this was a serious matter of self-defense. If I was going to defend myself and the universe against Alien-Bot, I was going to need some serious firepower.

Although I didn't know Sven, I'm sure he would understand about the upgrades. He probably also knew about a bunch of other stuff we could use to help defeat Alien-Bot. I was so worried that Mommy and Daddy were going to say no to the upgrades that I thought about asking them to take me to Sven's just for a checkup and then secretly giving him the drawing. But that would be dishonest, and I already knew that being sneaky and dishonest almost always backfires and causes a bigger mess than the original problem was. So I decided to be honest and tell them that I needed to talk to them about my cyborg stuff but that I didn't know to say it in a way they could understand and that Sven might be able to help explain it.

"It's important," I told them. "I have something to show you, but I don't want to show it to you until we're at Sven's."

"Why not?" Mommy asked. "Do you feel sick?"

"Are you growing any extra toes or arms or another head?" Daddy asked. I thought he was kidding at first, but he looked and sounded totally serious.

"No, it's nothing like that," I said. "I just don't know how to explain it. But Sven might be able to help me explain because he knows about this stuff. *Please?* It's very very *very* important to me!"

Mommy and Daddy looked at each other and nodded.

"Okay, bud," Daddy said. "Maybe we can go down there on Saturday morning. Do we need an appointment?"

"I'll send him a message now," I said, and just like that my cyborg video screen that only I could see turned on and composed a message to Sven:

DEAR SVEN: THIS IS HYPERKID. CAN I COME TO YOUR GARAGE ON SATURDAY MORNING?

A few seconds later I received a response:

DEAR HYPERKID: THIS IS SVEN. OF COURSE YOU CAN COME TO MY GARAGE ANY TIME. NO APPOINTMENT NECESSARY. I HAVE BEEN EXPECTING YOU.

"Sven says Saturday morning is fine," I said. "Thank you for your understanding."

Mommy and Daddy looked at each other again, and then Daddy looked back at me.

"I'm proud of you, Bud," he said. "It seems like you have really thought about this and figured out what you need to do. I'm also glad to see that you're not afraid to ask for help. Sometimes asking for help is a much more difficult than it should be."

CHAPTER 3

From the outside, Sven's Garage looked like a typical auto mechanic's shop. It was an old building not very big with a single garage door and an office next to it, and there were a couple of broken down cars in the parking lot. Only the beat up old sign above the front door gave any clues that this shop may be a bit different because there was an old Viking ship on it and an alien wearing a Viking hat. The sign also had a Swedish flag, which Daddy would like.

"That's a cool sign," Daddy said as he pulled the car into the lot. Mommy and I looked up at the sign, but Parker didn't look and kept playing with one of my old Hot Dog Guy action figures he had brought with him.

There was one empty spot in the lot, so Daddy pulled in and turned the car off. I was

really nervous by now, and suddenly I wasn't so sure that this was a good idea. I had counted on Sven taking my side, but now the fear that he might not was starting to take over. It suddenly felt like my entire future as a super hero was on the line. While everyone else took their seat belts off and opened the doors, I just sat there.

"Are you alright, bud?" Mommy asked when she noticed that I hadn't gotten up.

"I'm fine," I said with my annoyed voice. Sometimes I get annoyed when people ask me how I'm doing when I'm not feeling that great. I looked out the window and saw Daddy already walking towards the office with Parker, who was holding his hand and excitedly talking about one of the missions he had played on *The Super Hero Super Video Game.* It made me feel a little better that they were going in first, so I finally unbuckled my seat belt and got out of the car.

There was no one inside the office, and the place was a mess. There was a desk covered with a pile of grease-stained auto manuals, small car parts, and a credit card terminal, and on top of the manuals there was a computer keyboard but no monitor. In one corner of the room there was a small customer waiting area that was just a few old chairs, a coffee machine, and a water cooler. Parker and I sat down while Mommy and Daddy looked around.

"Hello?" Daddy called out. "Anyone home?"

A few moments later the door that led to the garage opened and a very old man walked into the office. He had long silver hair and a long silver beard and he looked like a wizard in a mechanic's uniform. His eyes were the brightest shade of blue I had ever seen and they were glowing, but he didn't look up at us while he was closing the door or when he was pulling out the desk chair to sit. His dark blue mechanic's shirt had a small white oval patch with "Sven" stitched on it in red letters.

After he was comfortably seated, he finally looked up and his glowing blue eyes instantly locked on me. For a split second I felt afraid, but the eyes must have had some kind of special powers because I suddenly felt relaxed.

"I have been expecting you," he said to me. His voice was smooth and calm, and he spoke with a slight accent. He then asked, "Where's the other one?"

Mommy and Daddy looked at each other with confused expressions.

"This is Morgan," Daddy said, patting my head. "And the little guy is Parker. These are the only two we have."

"I did not mean your youngest child," Sven said, "although he may eventually come to see me someday when he has grown a little more. I meant the other one. The red one."

"You mean Brian?" I asked.

"If Brian is the red one, then yes, that is the one I mean," Sven said.

"He's not here," I said. "It's just me. I'm the green one."

"Very well," Sven said. "He too will come see me eventually."

After an uncomfortably long silence, Daddy finally spoke up.

"Morgan said he needed to talk to you—and us—about something," he said.

Sven didn't look at Daddy and kept his eyes locked on me. I wasn't scared, but I didn't know what to say. Before I realized what I was doing, I stood up and took the drawing out of my pocket. I unfolded the paper and held it out for Sven. He continued looking at me as he reached across the desk and took the drawing from my hand. He then leaned back in his chair and started looking at it.

"Yes," he whispered. "Yes."

He then handed the drawing back to me and pressed a button on his keyboard. Suddenly a holographic monitor appeared on the desk, which was absolutely the coolest thing I had ever seen.

"Can we get one of those?" I asked Mommy and Daddy, but they didn't answer.

"The boy must be scanned," Sven said.

"Scanned?" Mommy asked worriedly. "What do you mean?"

"I can see the concern in your eyes," Sven said, his glowing eyes now fixed on Mommy.

"I can assure you that no harm will come to the boy, nor will any privacies be violated. This particular scan is similar to an x-ray, only without the harmful radiation, and it is designed to inspect his cyborg parts and human bones, but nothing more."

Mommy suddenly looked very relaxed, but I could tell that Daddy was getting upset.

"Hey, guy, why are you looking at my wife like that?" Daddy said. "And who do you think you are scanning my son?"

Sven then looked at Daddy, which made him suddenly appear relaxed. Then, without saying anything else, Daddy walked around Sven's desk and began staring at the painting on the wall of an old Viking ship that looked similar to the one on the sign out front. The

ship had a giant trident at the front of it and a huge one-eyed octopus sitting on the back that almost looked alive and seemed to follow you if you moved your head around.

"As I was saying," Sven said to Mommy, "I can assure you that no harm will come to your son from the scan. I can also assure you that he was correct in coming to see me."

"Are you a wizard?" Parker asked. "You look like the wizard from *Blockos Galactic Super Hero League Ultimate Building Blocks Omniverse*."

Usually adults think Parker is being cute when he says stuff like that, but Sven looked dead serious when he answered.

"I can assure you, young man, that I am no wizard," he said to Parker. "I am merely a highly skilled mechanic from another land. At one time I was an explorer, but I have since retired from that profession."

Sven then looked back at me and suddenly everything in the room turned blue. A skeleton appeared on the holographic monitor that looked like a professional version of my drawing. There was a scanner on the forehead and a transformation bone on the sternum, and both were highlighted in red. My cyborg arm looked pretty much the same on the monitor as it did in real life, but there was a piece highlighted in red where the weapon transformation bone would be.

Suddenly the monitor disappeared and the colors in the room turned back to normal.

"It is as I suspected," Sven said to me. "You are already equipped with the scanner and both transformation bones. The transformation bones are special types of bones that are both mechanical and organic. The structural transformation bone built into your sternum controls transformations into other beings. The weapon transformation bone built into your cyborg arm controls weapon transformations, which consist of different kinds of blasters such as fire, ice, repulsor rays, sound waves, and a few others. Both the structural and weapon transformation bones are fueled by hyperactive energy, which you possess in higher levels than most other humans your age. This is likely why you and the red one were detected by the meteors that transformed you, as the ability to harness and utilize hyperactive energy is useful technology in some civilizations, and the natural ability to produce this energy is considered very valuable. These abilities are already built into your cyborg mainframe, but they just need to be switched on. I'm not really sure why they are switched off now, but I suppose Alien-Bot had a reason for this, or perhaps there was a malfunction of some kind. But activation is a relatively simple matter."

"So, it *is* true that Alien-Bot turned us into cyborgs," I said. "I knew it!"

"It is true," Sven said. "He is the one that sent out the meteors, and I believe that the reason for his visit last year was to check up on you and the red one to make sure that your transformations into cyborgs were successful."

"Wait, hold on a minute," Mommy said. "Transformation powers and blasters? Alien-Bot? Morgan, what is he talking about? What was on that paper you showed him?"

I was expecting Daddy to add something to the conversation, but he was still staring at the painting and seemed to be in a trance.

Sven then looked at me and said, "I see that you have not showed your drawing to your parents or discussed any of this with them."

"I didn't know how to explain it!" I said.

"Please remain calm," Sven said.

"Sorry," I said. "I thought you could help them understand. I need these powers."

"You are a very wise boy," Sven said. "I was expecting you to be more impulsive, but I can tell that you have given this a great deal of thought. It is very wise to think before you speak or act."

Dr. Popsicle had often used the word "impulsive" when speaking about my behavior. Because I am hyperactive, sometimes I just start doing stuff before my mind even realizes what it is doing. He said my mind would eventually become faster and more able to control my actions before they happen, but for now I have to take medicine that helps me stay calm and not act so impulsive.

"Why do you *need* these powers?" Mommy asked me.

"Because Alien-Bot is coming back," I said. "I can feel it."

"He is speaking the truth, Mrs. Wallace," Sven said. "Your son is having premonitions."

"What does that mean?" I asked.

"It means that you subconsciously know that something is going to happen," Sven said. "In this case, I think you realize that Alien-Bot will soon return and that you are not yet prepared. You also realize that you have these powers within you and that you will need them to defend yourself against him."

"I don't like the sound of this," Mommy said, starting to look and sound upset again, but Sven looked at her and she calmed down.

"I believe that this is all part of a plan hatched by Alien-Bot to recruit an army of cyborg soldiers that will help him carry out his plans to destroy the universe," Sven said. "What I know of Alien-Bot is that he was once a great scientist and explorer, but something caused him to go mad. I believe that he sent out these meteors to transform intelligent beings into cyborgs that he can control. Honestly, I am a bit puzzled as to why he has not already taken control of your son's cyborg system and why the transformation abilities are switched off. I have a feeling that this was not intentional. It is likely that Alien-Bot will eventually discover this malfunction and correct it, which would then allow him to assume control of your son's cyborg system and take control of his human mind."

"Can't we just remove Morgan's cyborg powers so that this Alien-Bot can't find him?" Mommy asked.

"No!" I cried. Sven looked at me with his glowing eyes and I calmed down a little, but I was still upset because I had been worried that Mommy was going to say something like this.

"Alien-Bot already knows who your son is," Sven said. "And he obviously knows how to transform a human into a cyborg. Even if we remove your son's cyborg powers, it is likely that Alien-Bot can still easily find him and simply transform him back. So, I think it would be safer for your son to keep his cyborg abilities and switch on the additional powers."

"How do you know all of this?" Mommy asked. "Who are you, really?"

"I am merely an old explorer who knows things about this universe that few other humans know," Sven said. "I also have a friend who knows of Alien-Bot. This friend warned me that something had happened to Alien-Bot that caused him to go mad and that he was now determined to destroy the universe. Unfortunately I have not been able to make contact with this friend for ten years, so I fear that something bad has happened to him. Without any further updates from my friend, I have had difficulty tracking Alien-Bot's whereabouts during the last decade until he showed up here on Earth last year. I have also studied some of the meteorite samples I gathered from the storm that transformed your son and his friend into cyborgs. They contain technology so advanced that it must have been created by Alien-Bot since he is one of only a few beings in the universe who knows how to create technology sophisticated enough to transform beings from their native selves into cyborgs. Obviously this technology is very dangerous, especially when possessed by a being who has lost his sanity."

"But what does all this have to do with my son?" Mommy asked. "There are plenty of hyperactive kids in the world. Why *him*?"

"That I do not know," Sven said. "Your son and his friend, and possibly another that I have been unable to track down, were exposed to these meteors."

"There's another one?" I asked excitedly.

"Possibly," Sven said. "I have not been able to confirm it. All I know is that if there is another, he or she is not currently situated in this local area. In any event, we cannot change the past, nor are these cyborg abilities transferable to another host. The bottom line is that your son and his friend are now cyborgs, and that Alien-Bot has plans for them."

"Isn't the government responsible for protecting us from stuff like this?" Mommy asked. "Can't we report this to someone?"

Sven stared at Mommy for a moment then let out a startling big belly laugh.

"Mrs. Wallace," he said. "Have you not been paying attention to the world around you? Today's politicians have no interest in spending the time or the money to protect us common citizens from actual threats. The only thing they care about is protecting themselves and those who have been loyal to them. They will attack anyone who opposes them. The only dangers they see are the threats to their own wealth and power. They don't care about you or I or the air we breathe. They lie by telling us that the real threat is our fellow human beings, and they lie by telling us that actual threats such as the destruction of our planet are hoaxes. Our own Mayor Martinez called Alien-Bot appearing in the wormhole last year a hoax created by the media, even though she was there and saw it with her own eyes. The whole city of West Plains was there. We all saw it with our own eyes. Numerous reputable scientists have already proven that it really happened, yet her loyal followers continue to support her statement that it was a hoax. You and I were there as well, Mrs. Wallace. We saw it with our own eyes. So I have to ask: Who are you going to believe? Are you going to believe your own eyes, or are you going to believe the mouths of politicians telling you that what your eyes are seeing right in front of you isn't real?"

Mommy looked at Daddy, but he didn't

seem to know what was happening.

"Do you really trust these politicians to protect your son, Mrs. Wallace?" Sven asked. "And do you trust them to do what is right in protecting all of us from the actual threats our civilization faces? I for one trust that you and your husband will do what is best to protect your son. I also trust that your ten your old son and his friend will do a better job protecting our world far more than I trust any of these unqualified clowns masquerading as government officials. Alien-Bot will be back, and your son will need to be prepared to defend himself. This is his only chance. This is *our* only chance. If he is not prepared, it will not only be his own life that is threatened. It is all of us, everywhere."

Mommy again looked at Daddy.

"Can you snap my husband out of that trance?" Mommy asked.

"I did not put him in that trance," Sven said. "In fact, I do not know why he has reacted to that painting in this way, and I do not know how to snap him out of it. Is your husband an old Viking by chance?"

"He says he is," Mommy said. "He tells a lot of crazy stories about his Viking ancestors, but I don't know if they're really true."

"He said his great great great great great great grandfather was once on a ship that was swallowed whole by a kraken, but he managed to escape when it let out a big belch," I said.

"That's just one of his ridiculous old sea yarns," Mommy said.

"Well, believe it or not, things like that did happen back then," Sven said. "Krakens are evil, I tell you, and the great white kraken Mopy Dink who ate my little pinky toe is still out there somewhere. I can feel his evil presence whenever I am near the sea. I have chased that kraken all over the world, and someday I will find him. So, anyway, those stories your husband tells may be true."

"Ugh," Mommy said.

"Those were some crazy times back then," Sven said. "If your husband does have Scandinavian characteristics like myself, he may have the ability to channel events that his ancestors experienced in the distant past. It certainly appears that something about that painting that has taken hold of his mind."

"Alright, never mind about him for now," Mommy said. "What do you think we should do about my son?"

"It would be wise to activate your son's structural transformation ability and the blasters on his cyborg arm," he said.

"But what is this 'structural transformation ability'?" Mommy asked.

"It is the ability to transform into a cyborg version of other living beings," Sven said. "This includes organic beings, as well as machines, which, as a mechanic, are near and dear to my heart. Machines are living beings too, although they often lack the level of consciousness that most organic creatures have—but we can share our consciousness with them. We can even give them their own intelligence, which some people call 'Artificial Intelligence'. But I do not agree with that term because the intelligence we give them is real. The structural transformation ability can also include beings from the creative mind, such as those you would find on television programs, movies, and video games."

"Cool!" I said.

"But how does this transforming happen?" Mommy asked.

"I can scan things with my scanner," I said, pointing to my forehead. "After I scan something, I can transform into it. I can turn into a cat or a dog or car or even Hot Dog Guy!"

"The transformation is something like a

disguise," Sven said. "No matter what your son transforms into, the real Morgan will still be in there. In fact, even the non-cyborg version of Morgan is still in there. It is in his DNA, which the cyborg system keeps on file. This is why I have the ability to transform him back to his normal non-cyborg self if he wants to. But I know that this is not what he wants because he became a cyborg one year ago, yet this is the first time he has come to see me."

"This is true," Mommy said. "He wanted to stay a cyborg and be a super hero. But what if he gets stuck in one of these 'disguises' and can't transform back?"

"I can help with that," Sven said. "Even when he is transformed, he will still be your son, and I can remove the disguise if necessary without harming him."

"Do you have super powers?" I asked Sven.

Sven smiled and said, "I have lived a long life and have learned a great many things along the way. But I was not born with special abilities, nor was I given them as you were. Everything I know how to do and all of the knowledge I possess are things that I have learned through experience and the teachings of others. If you keep an open mind and take advantage of the things that this amazing universe has to offer and do everything you can to learn how it works, you too can achieve a great many things. And if you take care of your mind and body, you can live a long, long time. Eating beets can also help. The longer you live, the more knowledge you will accumulate. So, you can only imagine how much knowledge I have accumulated over a thousand years."

"You're a thousand years old?" I asked.

"A little older than that," Sven said with a smile. "Do you see that painting that has so captured the attention of your father? That is my old ship, the *Universal Explorer*, that I sailed to Greenland in the year 982. I built that ship myself using common hand tools. It took me ten years to build, but she was a fine sturdy ship. I even sailed her all the way to North America long before Columbus ever got there and buried some treasure on Oak Island up in Nova Scotia. Believe it or not, she's still out there, only now she's a space vessel."

"You turned it into a spaceship?" I asked in amazement.

"Not me," Sven said. "A friend of mine. The same friend I spoke of earlier. We actually made a trade. I gave him the ship, and he showed me how to turn it into a space vessel using highly advanced alien tech. I loved that ship more than anything and it was really difficult to give her up, but I knew that the knowledge would be more valuable. Knowledge is far more valuable than material possessions, even though I later realized that the *Explorer* was more than just a material possession to me—it was my home. But I have no regrets, and now this garage is my home. The knowledge has served me well."

"Ship," Daddy mumbled, still staring at the painting.

"So, you really can't fix my husband?" Mommy asked.

"No," Sven said. " But I am sure he will eventually snap out of it. Maybe."

"Getting back to this blaster business," Mommy said. "I'm very concerned that he is actually going to have a weapon on his arm that can really hurt someone. The little laser blaster he has now is fine because it can't really hurt anyone. But I don't want my son to be walking around with dangerous illegal weapons attached to his body."

"I certainly understand that, Mrs. Wallace," Sven said. "I am not an expert on the law, but I do not believe that there are any laws on the books that ban defense mechanisms with inherent organic qualities or alien tech. So I do not believe that the blasters would be illegal. And since your son's cyborg system is not yet under Alien-Bot's control, I can program the blasters not to function if they are pointing at humans or other creatures of earth—except maybe krakens. I will also attempt to build a firewall to try and keep Alien-Bot from gaining control, but he is a master hacker and would probably be able to get around it fairly easily."

Sven then looked at me and said, "Getting back to the krakens, they are vile creatures, the bullies of the sea. Fortunately none have been spotted in Earth's waters for centuries, but be ready to blast if you see one."

"My fourth grade teacher Mrs. Crabcake is part kraken," I said.

"Ah, yes, I know Esther Crabcake quite well," Sven said, his face turning pink. "Her and I go back quite a ways. But that's another story for another day. You won't be able to blast her since she is part human, and a fine lady of the sea as well."

Sven's face was now bright red and his

glowing blue eyes started flickering. I looked at Mommy and was surprised to see that she had a little smile on her face.

"Yes, well, ahem, what were you saying?" Sven asked, still a bit distracted.

"What about my fire armor?" I asked, wanting to make sure that I didn't forget to mention it. "The only time it deployed was during the fire at school last year. Can you unlock that so I can control when it deploys?"

"Of course," Sven said.

I was expecting Mommy to say something about the fire armor, but she seemed to be deep in thought—although it wasn't as bad as the trance that Daddy was still in.

"Can we go now?" Parker asked. "I want to go home and play video games."

"That is a wise idea, young one," Sven said. "The universe may need your abilities someday as well."

Mommy suddenly snapped to attention.

"What was that?" she asked worriedly.

"That question will be answered in time," Sven said. "But for now, Mrs. Wallace, you and your husband have much to discuss. If you decide to allow me to activate your son's dormant abilities, come back next week at this time. And Morgan, please tell the red one to come see me. This is of great importance."

Sven then looked at Daddy.

"And, one more thing, Mrs. Wallace," he said. "I strongly suggest that you drive your vehicle back to your home, as Mr. Wallace does not seem fit to do so himself at the moment."

CHAPTER 4

On our way home I transmitted a message to Brian about going to see Sven, and he replied by thanking me for the useful information and suggesting that I read this fascinating article about axiomatic quantum field theory. I have no idea what that is or how to even pronounce it, and even Mommy said she never heard of it—and she went to one of those super smart colleges that has old buildings with ivy on the walls. Daddy was still in a trance, but he did mumble the name "Hawking", which Mommy said was probably a reference to Stephen Hawking, who is one of the smartest guys in the world and whose books Daddy has read. But for Brian to read something like this made me further suspect that he was attempting to develop hyper-intelligence as a new super power. Mommy said that knowledge is the greatest super power of them all, but I still think flying would be better.

Daddy didn't snap out of his trance until about dinner time. He said the last thing he remembered was staring at the Viking ship painting in Sven's office and having a dream about discussing axiomatic quantum field theory with Stephen Hawking and Brian.

After Parker and I went to bed, Mommy and Daddy had a long discussion about whether or not they should allow Sven to turn on my transformation abilities and weapon blaster. Even though I have super hearing, the "eavesdrop rule" they created in my cyborg system to keep me from listening to their private conversations prevented me from hearing what they said.

I had trouble falling asleep that night and did a lot of twisting and turning in bed because I was expecting them to say no. So I was totally surprised in the morning when they told me that they were going to allow Sven to activate my transformation and blaster abilities because I needed a way to defend myself against Alien-Bot. They made a condition that I could not show or tell anyone about these abilities except for Brian, which made sense because super heroes don't want their enemies to know about all their powers so that they can catch them off guard when they need to. Mommy had also looked into the legal part of it and was now convinced that the blasters wouldn't be illegal because the blaster itself would be part of my anatomy and would be fueled by my natural hyperactive energy. But she wasn't so sure about the transformation abilities because if I transformed into a car or a truck, I would probably have to register myself with the Department of Motor Vehicles. But she said there may be a legal loophole because I would only be disguised as a vehicle and would still actually be myself, but this would be difficult to prove in a court of law because I would still be able to perform exactly like a real vehicle.

"This would be a sketchy legal defense," she said, "but the safety of my son is more important than any legal gray areas, and this is an unprecedented case where his personal safety and the safety of Earth, the Milky Way, and the entire universe is in peril and our government is not willing to do what it takes to defend us because they are too busy fighting with each other instead of fighting for the people they are supposed to be working for!"

Daddy leaped off the couch and started clapping big and cheering, and I started cheering and clapping too because I now knew for sure that I would be getting the new powers. Parker also paused his video game for a moment and started clapping, and Ralston started meowing and purring loudly.

While I was very excited about getting my upgrades, I spent the next few days worried that Mommy and Daddy would suddenly change their minds because they seemed more worried and serious than usual. This was like the feeling I get just before Christmas when I'm really excited about getting my presents, but at the same time I become so worried that I'm not going to get everything I asked for that I sometimes get sick and throw up in bed while trying to fall asleep on Christmas Eve. I was also worried that Alien-Bot would show up before I got the upgrades on Saturday morning, so I was pretty stressed out when I wasn't busy doing stuff.

Fortunately my group at the WPYC summer camp did some cool stuff during that week to keep me distracted. First we went to CrazyLand, the local amusement park with the rickety old rides that are scarier than the rides at the big amusement parks because you really do feel like you might die. Then we went to Danny Mustard's, the arcade where you win tickets for playing games and use them to buy prizes at the counter on your way out. I only had enough tickets to win a little rubber ducky dressed as a ninja, which I probably would have liked more last summer when I was nine, but I was ten now, so I gave it to Parker.

When Saturday finally came and we went back to Sven's, I asked him if he had heard from Brian. He said that he had and that his upgrades were complete, and now it was my turn. Mommy then asked Sven if he was going to have to put me under. I didn't know what that meant, but Daddy explained that sometimes they have to put you to sleep before surgery. But Sven laughed.

"Of course not!" he said. "I am not making any modifications to his human side. I only need to upload some code into his cyber system and then run some diagnostic tests to make sure everything is active and working properly. I could do it remotely, but for security reasons I prefer to do it directly from this special offline chip I built in my lab. Basically, I just have to plug it into his cyborg arm and the code will upload in a minute."

"You have a lab?" I asked.

"Of course," Sven said. "But unfortunately I cannot show you that. There are some highly sensitive things in there, and the location is top secret. I wear a cloaking device whenever I go there so that nobody can track my location."

"What's a cloaking device?" I asked.

"It's something that makes you physically and digitally invisible," he said.

"Cool!" I said. "Can you also install a cloaking device for me?"

Sven laughed and said, "I don't think your parents would approve. Besides, I would need some time to build it. Maybe at some other time I can whip one up that can make you invisible to everyone except your parents."

"Cool!" I said, although I was disappointed about still being visible to Mommy and Daddy.

"Anyway," Sven said, "right now let's focus on today's installation. In terms of pain, you have nothing to worry about. You will not feel a thing. I'm sure your experiences up the street at Dr. Popsicle's office are far more painful with his needles and tongue depressors. All I have to do is insert this chip into the housing of your cyborg arm and the code will start installing automatically."

Sven opened his desk drawer and took out a small transparent case that held the chip, which was about the size of a fingertip and was glowing bright neon green.

"Is that alien tech?" Daddy asked.

"It is, but I built it using the knowledge my friend gave me," Sven said. "This is why I truly believe that knowledge is much more valuable than material possessions such as my ship. Although I miss that old ship dearly, the knowledge I acquired has allowed me to build far more impressive things such as this chip. This alien tech really is quite remarkable. I've come a long way from building old wooden Viking ships using common hand tools."

Sven then asked me to lift my cyborg arm. After I did so, he plugged a wire into a small hole near my elbow that I never realized was an input jack. The wire was connected to his computer, and he typed something that caused a flap on my arm to suddenly pop open and reveal a control panel with several ports.

"Are those USB ports?" Daddy asked.

Parker laughed and said, "Those aren't USB ports! Silly Daddy!"

"Now, please stay as still as possible," Sven said to me. He then put the chip case on his desk and carefully opened it. He began staring at the chip intensely and his already glowing blue eyes started getting brighter. But after nothing happened for a minute or so, Daddy asked Sven if he was okay.

"Sir, I need complete silence in order to focus," Sven said.

"That's a cool painting over there," Mommy said. Daddy looked over at the Viking ship painting on the wall and mumbled the word "ship", then slipped into a trance like he had done last week. Sven looked at Mommy.

"He would have just kept interrupting you," Mommy explained.

"Thank you, Mrs. Wallace," Sven said. He then resumed staring at the chip, and after a couple of minutes it began to slowly float shakily upwards. He continued to stare at it intensely until it stabilized and started floating towards the panel on my arm. When it was above the panel, it began to descend until it suddenly got sucked into one of the ports as if it had been pulled by a powerful magnet.

Sven then started typing on his keyboard and the same image scan of my skeleton from last week appeared on the holographic monitor. He spent a few minutes checking the diagnostics before finally typing something that caused the flap on my arm to close and lock.

"You can open the flap on your interface in the event of an emergency," Sven told me. "Otherwise, you should leave it closed at all times. Do not play with this or modify it in any way. Now we need to go down to the basement to test the blaster. I have set up a blaster range down there where you can safely test the upgrades. Mrs. Wallace, I suggest you stay here to watch the little one and your husband. I will turn on the monitor so you can watch from here."

Sven then pointed a remote at the flatscreen TV up on the corner of the wall and changed the channel to one that showed a large empty basement space with some kind of figure in the corner that looked like Alien-Bot with bullseye targets on it.

"I don't want him doing anything dangerous," Mommy said.

"I can assure you that the boy will be fine," Sven said. "It will be far more dangerous if I don't show him how to use the blasters."

I followed Sven through the door that led to the garage. At the back of the garage there was a freight elevator big enough to fit a car, so if there wasn't a car up on the lift you could drive right into the garage and straight through to the elevator.

As we slowly descended down to the basement, Sven said, "I don't want you to test the transformation abilities now. When you get home later, try to test it on your own when your mother isn't looking. The shock of seeing her son turn into another being might be too much for her to handle. But I am confident that it will work just fine. If there are any problems, you can just send me a message and I should be able to fix the problem remotely."

The basement was much larger than it looked on the TV up in the office. In addition to the Alien-Bot target, there were a couple of beat up old cars in one corner, one of which looked like it had been set on fire.

"This is a fortified bunker down here," Sven said. "The walls cannot be destroyed. But we will still only be testing your blasters on low power and shooting at the target."

Sven pointed to the life-sized model of Alien-Bot with a bullseye target on its head and another on its chest. It was motionless, but it looked so real that it was hard to tell that it wasn't really alive. Sven noticed my look of concern.

"Unlike the real Alien-Bot, this one is just a dummy," he laughed. "It is not alive. Now, what you need to do first is deploy the blaster by saying 'deploy arm blaster', or just start thinking it until the words appear on your cyborg screen."

Knowing that I didn't have enough patience at the moment to use thought commands, I said "Deploy arm blaster". Suddenly my fire armor deployed, except now instead of the bulky fire extinguisher on my left arm, there was what looked like a small cannon. The transformation was smooth and quiet except for a few metal clicks and clacks that echoed through the basement. The only other time my fire armor was deployed was during the classroom fire last year, which was such a crazy intense situation that I barely remembered that transformation process.

I lifted my cannon arm and pointed it at the Alien-Bot dummy. I was expecting it to be heavy, but it was only a little heavier than my regular cyborg arm. A target with crosshairs appeared on my cyborg screen, and off to the side there was a list of different things that could be blasted: fire, ice, wind, slime, lava, sonic waves, repulsor rays, magnetic waves, a power bomb, and fire extinguisher foam.

"The same blaster is used for all of the elements," Sven said. "It can also be used as a fire extinguisher, so you no longer have that bulky fire extinguisher anymore. Basically, you just have to focus on the name of the element on the list that you want to use until it turns red and starts blinking, or you can just say out loud 'activate ice blaster' or whichever one you want to use. You can always just say the commands out loud if you are having difficulty focusing. After activating the blaster, you then locate your target, and it will tell you when you are locked on. A fire button will then appear on the screen that you can focus on for a full second, or you can just say 'fire'. When you are out of danger, you can give the command to power down and retract the blaster, but your fire armor will remain deployed until you give a separate command to retract it. You now have control of your fire armor so that you can deploy or retract it any time by giving a command, but it will still automatically deploy if your cyborg system determines that there is danger. Additionally, I have upgraded your fire armor so that it is now also a pressurized suit that can feed you oxygen, so you can use it as a space suit if necessary."

"Cool!" I said. "Do you think I'll get to go to outer space?"

"In this case, hopefully not," Sven said. "But you must be prepared for all possibilities because we do not know what Alien-Bot is going to do. Anyway, I think I have covered everything, but do you have any questions?"

"I think I got it," I said.

"Then why don't you test it out?" Sven said. "Start with the fire blaster, then do the ice. But don't do any of the others."

"What about the slime?" I asked hopefully.

"Definitely not," Sven said. "I don't want to spend the rest of the day cleaning up such a mess."

"What about the power bomb?" I asked.

"No no NO!" Sven said. "That one should only be used in the most dire of situations. Just stick to the fire and ice for now. Understood?"

"Yes, sir," I said.

I looked at the target and aimed my blaster arm towards it. My heart was racing. I then looked at the menu of blast choices, but I was unable to focus on "FIRE BLASTER" long enough for it to start blinking red.

"You are not focused enough," Sven said. "When this happens, what should you do?"

"Activate fire blaster!" I said. The "FIRE BLASTER" menu text started blinking red and the target crosshairs appeared on my screen. I adjusted my aim until it locked on the target.

"Fire!" I shouted.

Suddenly a stream of fire shot out of the cannon and struck the target. The stream was easy to control, and I didn't feel the heat at all.

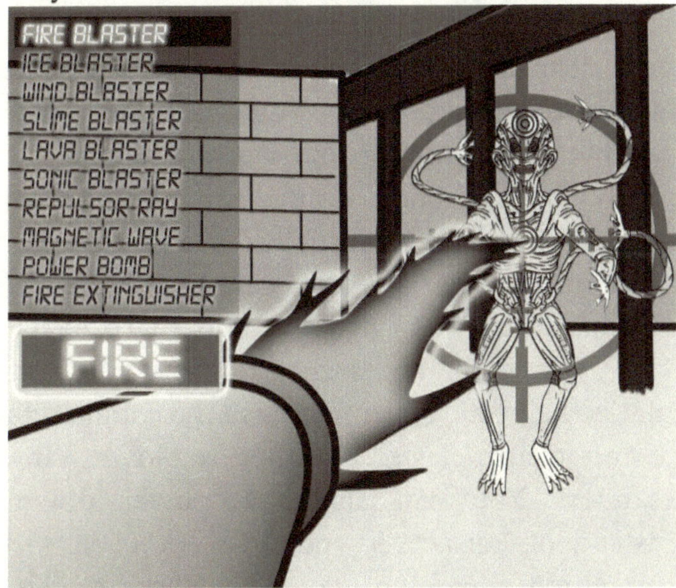

The metal on the Alien-Bot dummy started glowing orange where the fire was heating it. After Sven instructed me to disengage, there was a black stain where the glow had been.

"Excellent," Sven said. "Now try the ice."

I looked at the menu and focused on "ICE BLASTER", and this time I was able to make the selection without using a voice command. I then locked the crosshairs onto the target and focused on the "FIRE" button until a stream of water started shooting out of my cannon arm like a fire hose. The water immediately turned to ice on contact, and in a matter of seconds the Alien-Bot dummy was trapped inside a thick block of ice.

"Now you are focused," Sven said. "It is very difficult to focus when you are trying to learn something new. You have to keep starting and stopping and starting again. But when you practice doing something long enough, you will eventually be able to do it without the interference of conscious thought, and here you will find clear and sharp focus. Now, I have one more thing to show you, and that is the healing scanner. Give the commands to 'retract arm blaster' and then 'deploy healing scanner'. You can also say 'power down' instead of 'retract' if you wish, or even say something your own way. The cyborg system is smart enough to figure out what you mean."

I gave the commands and a glowing green circle appeared on the palm of my cyborg hand. I could hear a slight humming sound, but the hum sounded like it was inside my cyborg system and not coming from the hand itself.

"This healing scanner can detect injuries and heal some of them like broken bones, torn muscles, and flesh wounds," Sven said. "It is a very basic prototype that I designed, but hopefully someday I can get it to cure diseases like cancer or heart disease, and maybe even bring someone back to life. Perhaps I will even be able to get it to heal the sickness that causes people to feel hatred and intolerance. That would be the greatest super power of them all, but that kind of power is the most elusive."

CHAPTER 5

On the way home from Sven's I tried to think of a way to test my transformation abilities without Mommy and Daddy knowing, but I was stumped. I knew I had to be careful and transform into something small because if I was inside the house and transformed into an elephant or a truck, they would probably know. That gave me the idea to make a rule in my cyborg system not to be able to transform into something that can't fit inside the house.

After we got home I went up to my room and started building something with my Blockos when Ralston wandered in and jumped up on my bed to take a nap. Suddenly I realized that he was the perfect test case to transform into since he was definitely small enough, and even if Mommy and Daddy saw me, they would think I was regular Ralston unless they saw both of us at the same time.

I closed my bedroom door and gave the command to "scan object". My cyborg screen turned on and everything in the room turned dark until the scanner recognized Ralston as a scannable object. Ralston turned bright green on the screen and the scanner locked onto him, then a prompt appeared and asked, "SCAN OBJECT?" I just said "yes", and a green laser beam started scanning Ralston. The scan took only a couple of seconds, and Ralston didn't seem to notice because he didn't move at all. Then another prompt appeared asking me to name the scan file, so I just named it "Ralston".

I listened for a moment to make sure that nobody was outside my door. When I was sure that the coast was clear, I took a deep breath and focused on thinking "Transform into Ralston" until the words appeared on my cyborg screen and started blinking. At first nothing happened, but then a moment later everything turned so bright that I was blinded. The next thing I knew I was down on the floor next to my bed, which suddenly looked humungous. Below me I saw Ralston's front paws on the floor, including his cyborg paw on the right, but they were now my paws. It had worked! I really was a cyborg cat!

I didn't really know what to do, so I took a small step forward to get used to moving around with a cat's body. It wasn't too difficult, and I must have had Ralston's instincts because I felt like I could easily leap up onto the bed like he always does. So I just leaped up there like it was nothing and landed perfectly balanced. It was a pretty amazing feeling because I felt weightless even though Ralston is a fat old cat.

What hadn't occurred to me was that Ralston might freak out if he saw me. I had landed right next to where he was napping, and he lifted his head up and started staring at with a very angry look on his face. I tried to tell him to stay calm, but all I could say was "meow". This made him even angrier and he hissed at me, which was not a good sign.

Even though Ralston was our lovable family pet, he was a very tough cat. Daddy once told me that he had hunted down a few mice in the old New York City apartment we lived in when I was little. They had adopted him from a rescue shelter in Harlem before I was born, and Daddy said that he was a tough little kitten from the streets before he turned into the lazy fat cat we now know and love. I believe it because even before Ralston became a cyborg cat, he was able to scare away cats who wandered into our yard just by looking at them from the window. They must be really terrified now that he's a cyborg because I haven't seen another cat in the yard since the first time I saw him point a laser beam at one of them with his cyborg eye.

I knew I had to act fast, so I tried to focus on giving the command to transform back into my regular self, but at this point focusing was pretty much impossible. Ralston was not only giving me a death stare, but he was now also crouched with his front legs down and hind legs up and whipping his tail around as if he was about to attack me.

Suddenly he took a swipe at me with his left paw, but my cat instincts caused me to leap off the bed before he made contact. My human instincts were still working as well because I wanted to open the door and run out, but I couldn't open it with my paws. Ralston then leaped at me from the bed, but I managed to jump out of the way just in time.

Ralston was relentless, chasing me all over the room and screeching angrily while I screeched in terror and tried to get away, both of us knocking books and toys off the shelves and my stuff flying all over the room as if a tornado was passing through. I eventually realized that I couldn't keep running and jumping forever, so I stopped at an open space on my floor and hissed at Ralston. This surprised him for a moment and he froze. I thought that maybe this scared him and he would back off, but suddenly he leaped at me with cyborg paw ready to strike and his mouth open like he was going to bite my head off.

I thought I was done for, but suddenly the bedroom door opened and Ralston changed direction in mid-air and scooted under the bed.

"What's going on in here?" I heard Daddy ask. I looked up and saw him and Mommy standing in the doorway and felt relieved that they had saved me just in the nick of time, but I had momentarily forgotten that I was still a cat. So when I tried to start explaining what had happened, a "meow" came out of my mouth.

"Ralston!" Daddy said to me. "Bad kitty! What on Earth are you doing in here?"

He then stepped into the room to pick me up, but he didn't have a chance before the real Ralston shot out from under the bed. He ran through Daddy's legs, past Mommy, and scampered up the attic stairs to get to one of his hiding spots. Mommy let out a scream and Daddy said, "*Two* Ralstons? Noooooooooo…" He then fainted and slumped to the floor.

Mommy looked at me and then down at Daddy on the floor. I could tell that she didn't really know what to do, but fortunately she decided to go into the bathroom to get a cup of water for Daddy. This gave me a few quiet seconds to focus long enough on giving the thought command to transform back into my regular self. Everything turned bright again, and a moment later I was sitting on the floor as my regular self. Mommy came back and gave me a quick look before pouring the cup of water on Daddy's face to wake him up.

"What happened?" Daddy asked when he came to.

"Our son apparently transformed into our cat," Mommy said.

"I'm sorry!" I said. I had that feeling inside like I was going to cry. "I just wanted to try out my transformation ability because I didn't get to do it at Sven's!"

"It's okay," Mommy said. "Are you okay?"

"Yes," I said.

"So the transforming works okay?" Daddy asked.

"Yes," I said.

"Okay, good," Mommy said. "But from now on, please only use it when you have to. And please be careful."

I was expecting them to give me a long talk and possibly some kind of threat about going back to Sven's to have the transformation ability switched off, but they didn't mention it again. Their silence only made the situation seem more serious, and once again I felt the heightened awareness that Alien-Bot was out there somewhere and might be heading towards Earth at that very moment. Maybe he was already here somewhere watching Brian and I and waiting for the right moment to strike.

This heightened awareness was now hovering over me like a storm cloud, and with each passing minute it seemed to be getting darker and darker like the storm was getting closer. It felt like torture knowing that something bad was going to happen but not knowing what it would be and not being able to do anything about it. I also had no idea when it was going to happen, and it got to the point where every few minutes I asked my cyborg system for the present location of Alien-Bot, but I always got the same response:

SPECIFIC LOCATION UNKNOWN. PRESENCE CURRENTLY NOT DETECTED IN MILKY WAY GALAXY.

The message would make me feel relieved for a moment, but then the bad feeling would start building up all over again. Eventually the fear started turning into frustration. I just wanted this to happen so that this feeling would go away. I was ready to face Alien-Bot and put an end to this darkness once and for all.

CHAPTER 6

Alien-Bot didn't appear before the end of the summer, so Mommy and Daddy kept reminding me to try not to think about it and just go about my life as if everything was perfectly normal. They even let me play video games more than usual and often gave me a few minutes of extra playtime after my bath. They also suggested that I not do any super hero stuff so that I wouldn't be reminded about it, so I didn't except for catching the next door neighbor's pet rabbit that had escaped from their yard.

So, even though there was a storm cloud above me all summer, the rain never came, and when I was busy I was able to forget about it for a while. I was able to enjoy celebrating my tenth birthday when Mommy and Daddy took us to Tsunami World, the big water slide park about an hour north of West Plains. And at camp we did a couple of musicals where all the different age groups had to sing different songs. The first one was *Aladdin*, and the second one was *Grease*. I'm not crazy about singing, and apparently neither is Parker, but it kept us busy. For the *Grease* song, his group had to sing "Tears On My Pillow," but he just stood there with a mad face and did the opposite movements of what all the other kids were doing. He stood up when everyone else crouched down, and he crouched down when everyone else stood up. Our group did "Grease Lightning", which I didn't mind because we got to wear these cool 1950s style sunglasses that we were allowed to keep afterwards.

Even though I wasn't crazy about camp, nobody there seemed to care that I was HyperKid or said anything to me about it, so there was nothing there to remind me about Alien-Bot. It was kind of weird because usually somebody recognizes me whenever we go somewhere around town like the store or the pool or the movies. But nobody ever said anything about it at camp, which was actually kind of nice.

Surprisingly, I didn't see Brian all summer. He didn't always respond to my messages, and when he did he would usually just say something about a "big project" that he was working on and that he would give me an intelligence briefing on it in a few days. But he never did.

During the last week of summer vacation we made our usual trip up to the Sparkling Timber Lake Resort and Mountain Spa, which is about a four hour drive north of West Plains. It's always fun up there, but on the way home I felt sad because I knew fifth grade would be starting in a few days. Parker would also be starting kindergarten, and since the elementary schools in West Plains only went up to fifth grade, this would be the only year in our lives that we would both be going to the same school at the same time.

While I was dreading the first day of school, there was one really good thing about this year. Mr. Cooldude, the most popular teacher in the school, was now going to be teaching fifth grade, and I had been assigned to his class. Back at the beginning of fourth grade I had wanted to transfer into his class to get away from Mrs. Crabcake, but that plan never really got off the ground. So I had that going for me, which was good.

Mr. Cooldude was originally from southern California, and when he was younger he was a champion surfer. Nobody was really sure why he had traded the sunny beaches of California for the cold winters and blazing hot summers of West Plains, but he was such a cool guy that nobody cared. I was curious about it, though, so I asked my cyborg system to run a check on him. To my surprise, the following message appeared:

BARRY COOLDUDE: CLAIREMONT HIGH SCHOOL / SAN DIEGO, CA. ****FILE CLASSIFIED**

On the morning of the first day of school, Mr. Cooldude walked into the classroom carrying his surfboard. He was wearing a flowery Hawaiian shirt, shorts, and sunglasses. Even though the other teachers were boring and dressed more professionally, they all seemed to like him too and tried to act cool when they were around him. Nobody except me seemed to think it was strange that he always drove his 1960 Corvette convertible with the top down and his surfboard sticking out from the passenger seat even when it was raining or snowing. The nearest ocean beach was over fifty miles away, yet he always looked like he was about to catch some waves. Maybe in his mind he was still in California, which made it seem all the more strange that he lived and worked in West Plains. His file being classified also made me wonder if this was some sort of brilliant disguise, yet at the same time I didn't really care because he was such a cool guy. Nobody else seemed to care either that he was from another place and was so different, which was perhaps the genius of it. But maybe this guy was just so comfortable with who he was that he made the people around him feel comfortable with who *they* were. Either way, I was so glad that he was my teacher that I almost didn't mind going to school, although I still would have rather stayed home and played video games.

"Good morning fifth grade dudes and dudettes!" he said when he walked into the classroom. He leaned his surfboard against the wall in the corner and then turned to face us.

"This year is going to be *totally* awesome!"

I didn't see Brian anywhere, which made me think that he must be in one of the other classes. But when Mr. Cooldude was doing attendance, he did call out Brian's name.

"Brian Bullini?" Mr. Cooldude said. "Hey, dude, are you out there somewhere?"

"Call me BullStein," said a voice from the doorway.

A moment later one of the most unbelievable sights I had ever seen walked into the classroom. The other kids gasped, and Mr. Cooldude said "Whoa".

At first it was hard to tell that it even was Brian. Instead of his usual sloppy hair, ripped jeans, and skull shirt, he was dressed like a classic nerd. His hair was neatly combed and parted down the middle. He was wearing a thick pair of glasses and a short sleeve button-down shirt with pens and pencils sticking out of the pocket (fortunately he decided against wearing a pocket protector).Yet the strangest thing may have been the tie he was wearing that had on it an image of Albert

Einstein's head with bullhorns sticking out of its sides.

"Gnarly disguise, BullBorg—I mean Stein!" Mr. Cooldude said.

"What disguise?" Brian asked.

"Right, dude, I get it," Mr. Cooldude said with a big wink. "Far out!"

Brian looked around the classroom for an empty seat. There was one in the front and one in the back. Brian once told me that he liked to sit in the back because it was easier to hide the fact that he wasn't paying attention, but today he chose the open seat up front.

Although Brian now looked like the kind of student that a teacher would love, he somehow got off on the wrong foot with Mr. Cooldude. When attendance was finished, Mr. Cooldude suggested we go around the room and share what our favorite activities were and what was the coolest thing we did over "summer vay-cay". He sat on his teacher's desk facing us and said he would start with himself and said that he liked to surf and listen to old rock & roll music, and that the coolest thing he did over the summer was trying to hunt down "the big one" while surfing the Banzai Pipeline on the North Shore of Oahu in Hawaii. While he was talking, Brian raised his hand.

"Yes, BullStein dude," Mr. Cooldude said.

"Can we skip this 'getting-to-know-you' nonsense and begin a more academic discussion?" Brian asked. "I have some questions about mathematical formalisms in quantum mechanics."

"Whoa, chill out, BullDude," Mr. Cooldude said, still smiling like he always did when he spoke. "Harvard is a few exits north of here. Why don't you tell us about yourself and what you did over the summer."

"My name is Brian Bullini, and I am in the process of acquiring all of the accumulated knowledge of humankind and beyond. I spent the summer downloading all the textbooks and white papers I could find online onto my internal hard drive. I actually had to have a higher capacity drive installed over the summer to continue my studies."

"Far out, BullDude!" Mr. Cooldude said.

"And please don't call me 'BullDude' or 'BullBorg'. I now wish to be known as 'BullStein'."

"Yes, sir, Mr. BullStein dude!" Mr. Cooldude said.

By lunchtime the smile had started to disappear from Mr. Cooldude's face, which almost never happened. Brian was driving him crazy correcting everything he said. Mr. Cooldude managed to keep his cool, but just before everyone got up to head to the cafeteria, he asked Brian to stay behind.

Brian didn't show up on the playground until halfway through recess. He headed towards the spot against the fence where he used to stand and scare the kids away when he first moved here. He even had his thumbs hooked on his pants pockets like he used to, but now he was staring straight ahead at nothing in particular. I went over to talk to him, but when I got close he held up his index finger to indicate that he wanted me to wait a moment. A few seconds later he looked at me.

"Hello, Morgan," he said. "I was just downloading some of Norbert Weiner's work on path integral formulation."

"What happened to you?" I asked.

"What do you mean?" Brian asked.

"I mean, you've turned into a completely different person. You used to be this cool tough guy, but now you're just a mean nerd."

"That's not a nice thing to say," Brian said.

"I'm sorry," I said. "But you were really rude to Mr. Cooldude, and he's like the greatest teacher of all time."

"He needs to brush up on his quantum

mechanics," Brian said.

"No, you need to stop being such a jerk!" I said. "Just because you suddenly became smarter than everyone else doesn't give you the right to act like the rest of us are idiots!"

Brian thought about this for a moment.

"Perhaps you are correct," he finally said. "My own mother said almost the exact same thing to me only a few days ago. My psychologist said that I may have reached what he calls 'the age of reason', which is when the youthful mind starts thinking more like an adult and less like a kid. Maybe that's true, because at the beginning of the summer I discovered that my mind was understanding things that I had never really even thought about before, and for the first time ever academic stuff like science and math started to seem interesting to me. And now that I have a cyborg database to store all of this knowledge, I started downloading books like crazy and am using the text-to-speech engine on my cyborg system to read them out loud in my mind almost all day and night. Maybe I have gone a little overboard, but I really do enjoy being smart. I had always felt stupid all my life, but I don't anymore. The intelligence was always inside me, but I think my hyperactivity was causing distractions that were preventing it from reaching the surface. Now it is finally breaking through."

I kind of understood what he was saying, and I wish I felt a little smarter too. My hyperactivity makes it difficult for me to pay attention in class and to sit still when Mommy and Daddy are helping me with my homework, so learning new stuff is usually harder for me than most other kids unless it is something I am already interested in. I also sometimes get annoyed when someone corrects one of my mistakes, and then I get mad at myself for making the mistake in the first place. But seeing Brian like this was not a good sign either.

"Sven said you went to see him and got the transformation ability and blaster switched on," I said.

"Yes," Brian said. "He's the one who also gave me the extra capacity on my hard drive."

"Alien-Bot is going to come back," I said.

"I am aware of this," Brian said. "This is why I'm trying to accumulate as much knowledge as I can. We cannot simply overpower Alien-Bot—we have to outsmart him. And that will be no easy task. He's the smartest guy in the universe, which is what makes him the most powerful."

"But that doesn't mean you should be mean to everyone else," I said.

"You are wise like your father," Brian said.

"*My* father?" I asked.

"And you are right," Brian continued. "Mr. Cooldude said I have developed a sort of 'Algernon Complex'. I asked him what that meant, and he said it was from the book *Flowers for Algernon*, where the main character Charlie had a really low IQ, then some scientists performed surgery on him that made him a genius. But when he became a genius, he became a different person and started acting like kind of a jerk. The people who liked him when he was dumb couldn't relate to him anymore, and the people he worked with who used to make fun of him became afraid of him and tried to get him fired. So I will try to be nicer and not be like Charlie."

Suddenly there was a loud explosion in the sky. At first I thought it was thunder, but when I looked up and saw the small black spot in the sky above the baseball diamond, I knew exactly what was happening.

"He's here," I said.

The black spot grew larger until it opened up to a full-sized wormhole like the one that

Alien-Bot had emerged from last year. Its walls were lined with blue lightning, and in the middle you could see a few dim stars. I knew it was only a matter of moments before Alien-Bot appeared—or so I thought.

Suddenly a strong force locked onto us that started lifting us slowly off the ground. We couldn't move our bodies and were only able to turn our heads to look around, but even that was difficult. I think I screamed, but I wasn't sure if any sound actually came out.

Slowly we rose high above the playground towards the wormhole, and everything became silent except for the static electricity sound of the lightning that lined the tunnel walls. I was terrified, but when I looked over at Brian, I saw him smiling.

Then I received a message on my cyborg screen from Brian:

HERE WE GO, HYPERKID. STAY CALM AND TELL YOUR FEAR TO SHUT UP BECAUSE WE HAVE WORK TO DO. SVEN SAID WE WILL WIN AS LONG AS WE BELIEVE IN OURSELVES.

CHAPTER 7

We were now up really high above the playground, probably higher than the top of the Freedom Tower. I was scared that if the force lifting us up suddenly disconnected, we would immediately fall to our deaths. Then a message appeared on my cyborg screen:

*** DEPLOY FIRE ARMOR ***

In a matter of seconds Brian and I were both covered with our newly upgraded and pressurized fire armor that would protect us in outer space—which I now realized is where we were going. I had been so stuck on the idea that Alien-Bot would be coming back to Earth that I hadn't considered the possibility that he would bring us to wherever he was. It also occurred to me that Brian and I were about to become the youngest astronauts ever, but unfortunately I wasn't able to enjoy the historical part of our journey because I wasn't sure if we were going to make it back home. But every astronaut in history probably had that same exact fear.

The static electricity sound became almost deafening as we entered the wormhole. At first I had been worried about being electrocuted, but the inside of the hole was actually much bigger than it looked from below, so we weren't in danger of touching the walls.

The light of our sun soon disappeared and it became very dark except for the blue glow of the lightning around us. I looked down at my armor and saw that my HyperKid "H" logo was glowing bright neon green, which was very cool. Then I looked over at Brian to see if his logo was lit up and it was, except that it

was no longer the classic BullBorg "B" but the new BullStein logo of Albert Einstein's head with the bullhorns. The logo looked funny enough to relax me for a moment.

A short time later I could tell that we were exiting the wormhole because the static electricity sound was becoming fainter and the blue lightning glow was becoming dimmer. Then suddenly there was a thunderous boom behind us followed by total silence. I was able to turn my head around just enough to see that the wormhole had disappeared and Earth was no longer visible. Where the wormhole had been, all I could see were gazillions of stars and galaxies shining amazingly bright, but in front of us there were only the same few dim stars that were visible from the wormhole. These dim stars now appeared to be at the end of a long tube we were now entering that was nearly invisible except for the faint red glow that surrounded it. It felt like we were leaving the universe behind and heading towards some dark cold place.

It was so quiet now that we didn't seem to be moving at all. The only way I could tell that we were actually moving was that the dim stars were slowly getting larger, although they didn't seem to be getting any brighter. Even when we got really close and passed right by them, they still weren't any brighter. While our sun is a bringer of life, these stars seemed to be a sign of death and looked like they were on their way to disappearing into the darkness forever.

The opening in front of us was now completely black, but the red glow of the tube surrounding us seemed to be getting brighter. Now that there wasn't anything to look at, my mind started drifting. I was having difficulty finishing my thoughts until I suddenly heard Brian's voice inside my helmet, which I hadn't realized was equipped with an intercom.

"Can you hear me?" Brian asked.

"Yes," I said, suddenly at attention. "Can you hear me?"

"Affirmative," Brian said.

"What?" I asked.

"Yes, I can hear you," he said.

"Do you think Alien-Bot can hear us?" I asked.

"I hope not," Brian said. "I just finished setting up an encrypted intercom channel so that we can talk to each other securely, which is why I didn't say anything until now. If Alien-Bot knew about it he could probably easily hack it, but this is the best I can do for now, so let's not worry about it."

"I'm really scared," I said.

"Try not to let your fear overpower you," Brian said. "Sven thinks we can defeat him, and I believe him. But you have to believe in yourself. If you truly believe in what you are doing, your fear will move aside. I know you can do this because you overcame your fear last year when you confronted me on the playground, and then you did it again when the classroom went on fire. Just try to focus on what you already know how to do and don't let the distractions stop you. "

"What if I don't know what to do?" I asked.

"When the moment arrives, your instincts

will guide you," Brian said. "I realize that this sounds like something Olaf Wanton Sharona would say in *Stellar Clashes*, but I think he's right. As for right now, there's nothing we can do. I know it feels like we should be doing something, but we have to keep that restless feeling in check and stay calm until the time comes. Right now just try to convince yourself that we can do this. I truly believe that we can, and so does Sven. You need to believe it too."

"Are you scared?" I asked.

"Yes," Brian said. "But because I truly believe that we can defeat him, my fear is not overpowering me. Also keep in mind that a little bit of fear is actually a good thing. It keeps you cautious and doesn't let you become overconfident, which is when you start taking unnecessary chances."

"But how can you be so sure that we can defeat Alien-Bot?" I asked.

"Because he's vulnerable," Brian said. "Even though he's still the most intelligent being in the universe, Sven said that he may be suffering some kind of mental illness that has robbed him of his ability to feel emotion or recognize it in others. He used to be able to feel emotion because he's still part organic, but the illness that has caused him to want to destroy the universe has also stripped him of his compassion, and this has weakened his instincts. Now he is only able to rely on technical intelligence, which makes him predictable. This is his weakness, and this is our advantage. We may not be as smart as him, but our instincts are strong, especially yours."

"*Mine?*" I asked, surprised.

"Of course!" Brian said. "Last year when everyone else in West Plains thought I was a bad guy bully, you were the only one who saw that I wasn't."

"At first I thought you were," I said.

"But your instincts told you to be nice to me anyway, even though your intellect may have been telling you to stay away," Brian said.

"I guess," I said.

"The point is," Brian said, "that in order to have good instincts, you need to have the right balance of emotion and intelligence. You can't just rely totally on one or the other. I realize now that I almost made the same mistake as Alien-Bot in thinking that having more intelligence was all I needed to win, but Mr. Cooldude reminded me that intelligence isn't everything. And Alien-Bot is way more intelligent than either of us are, so we can't simply outsmart him. We have to use our instincts, and yours are way better than mine."

"With my instincts and your intelligence, we make a pretty strong team," I said.

"Exactly."

I thought about all this for a moment and realized that maybe he was right about my instincts being better than his. Brian did make poor decisions sometimes, like scaring the kids away on the playground last year and being rude to Mr. Cooldude this morning. Even his newfound intelligence couldn't stop him from being rude to the greatest teacher in the world. Before this morning, though, I could tell that something wasn't right with him. This feeling went back all the way to the beginning of the summer. I guess my instincts were trying to tell me something. Still, I wish I had at least a little bit more intelligence so that math and spelling wouldn't seem so difficult!

"How did you get so smart?" I asked. "Did the red meteor rays give you extra intelligence?"

"No," Brian said. "That's what I thought at first too, but Sven said that the meteor rays had nothing to do with it. He said that whatever intelligence I had was always there on the human side, and that the cyborg side only gives us the extra advantage of storing information on a hard drive that is directly accessible by our brains—but our ability to understand and use this information is all human and not artificial intelligence. Like I said earlier, my psychologist said that I may have reached 'the age of reason', perhaps a little earlier than most other kids. It may happen to you soon too. But for me it all started when we were working for Mayor Martinez. It really bothered me that she and her colleagues were treating us like dumb kids who couldn't understand what was really going on in our city, which is kind of the way they treat their own constituents. But it didn't take long for me to realize that they didn't care at all about governing and that they really weren't as smart as they thought they were. The only thing they were good at was winning elections, and their only concern was to make sure they got re-elected. I started to understand what my mother was saying about how the government wasn't doing anything to help her as a single mother who was holding down three jobs just so we could buy food and pay the rent in our dumpy old house. I heard other people in our neighborhood saying similar things, yet when I tried to talk to Mayor Martinez about it, she would cut me off and say she would look into it. So I started reading the news websites and then reading books about politics and realized that I not only understood it, but that I understood it better than these arrogant fools running our city who didn't care about anyone but themselves. So I started reading more, and soon reading became an obsession. I began devouring as many books as I could by downloading them onto my hard drive. But now I know that I went a little too far with it because it upset my balance. I think I'm okay now. Mr. Cooldude gave me a bit of a wakeup call. The guy really is a good teacher even if he isn't an expert on quantum mechanics."

We continued to float for what seemed like a really long time. My mind started drifting again whenever I wasn't talking to Brian, and I was starting to feel tired. Then it suddenly occurred to me that Mommy and Daddy would be really worried about me, so I decided to send them a message:

DEAR MOMMY AND DADDY, WE ARE IN OUTER SPACE. WE ARE OK. I AM NOT SCARED. LOVE, MORGAN

After I sent the message, the word "SENDING" kept blinking on the screen over and over again. Eventually it stopped and another message appeared saying that the estimated arrival time for the message was 45 billion years.

"I think there's something wrong with my message transmitter," I said to Brian. "It said that the message I just sent to my parents will get there in 45 billion years."

"That may be correct," Brian said. "The wormhole closed and we've already come out the other side. If it was still open, I think the message would be going through normally. Given that 45 billion light years is the distance estimated to be the edge of the observable universe from Earth, I think we have reached the end of the universe. Actually, those dim stars we just passed may have been the end. That was probably the oldest part of the universe, which is dying. Right now this tube we are in may be passing through a part of the universe that is already dead. It might be some sort of passageway that is leading us outside the universe."

"*Outside* the universe?" I asked as a new fear started to creep over me. "How is that possible?"

"I don't know," Brian said. "We may be going to a place where all the laws of our universe may not apply."

My head was starting to hurt as it tried to make sense of what was happening. At one point I started to feel like I was going to throw up until Brian said, "Look, up ahead! There's a star!"

Sure enough, straight ahead in the darkness there was a small red point of light. Unlike the stars we had just passed, this one seemed to be shining brightly.

"This is strange," Brian said. "All the other stars have died off here, yet this one has somehow managed to survive."

"Are we still in the universe?" I asked.

"I don't know," Brian said. "I don't think anything can exist in a void, so we must still be in the universe—unless we just entered a *different* universe. But I think it's more likely that this is what's left of an old galaxy in our universe that somehow managed to survive."

The red glow of the tube around us seemed to be getting wider until it eventually opened up to a clearing. It appeared that the tube expanded into a huge bubble that went all the way around the other side of the star. The bright red glow of the star itself against the darkness reminded me of the sad red glow of neon signs in the windows of closed stores whenever we drove through downtown West Plains on our way home from somewhere late at night.

"The star is a red giant," Brian said. "This is what our sun is going to become in about five billion years or so when it starts running out of fuel. It's going to turn red and start growing larger and larger. It will scorch everything and then engulf all the planets, and then it will eventually collapse and become a white dwarf star that looks nothing like our sun and leave no sign that Earth or the other planets were ever there. When the white dwarf cools, its carbon will crystallize into a giant diamond."

"Our sun is going to become a giant diamond someday?" I asked.

"Yep."

"Cool!" I said.

"But we won't be around to see it unless I have a breakthrough on the immortality project I'm working on," Brian said.

"The what project?" I asked.

"The immortality project," Brian said. "I'm working on something that will hopefully allow us to live forever. I haven't gotten that project off the ground yet, but I'm preparing a proposal for some venture capitalists out in Silicon Valley to fund the work."

I knew we must have been getting close to the star because it was getting larger at a faster rate, and soon a small dot appeared on the face of it.

"What is that black dot on the star?" I asked.

"It's a transit!" Brian said excitedly. "There's a planet crossing in front of it!"

Suddenly a robotic female voice that sounded like Zori from Mommy & Daddy's smartphones started talking through our intercoms:

Welcome to the Estarna Galaxy, the oldest galaxy in the known universe and current host to the Red-Gwot solar system. Red-Gwot is a red giant star with a single planet in its orbit named Alania. Alania is the native home of the Bot species, a highly intelligent civilization of cyborgs that have mostly abandoned the planet and moved elsewhere. Red-Gwot is the oldest living star in the universe, and Alania the oldest inhabited planet. This solar system would have likely died many millions of years ago, but the Bots managed to preserve it using their advanced matter containment technology. Thank you for using WikiGwot.

"Cool, they have their own wiki!" Brian said.

Our momentary distraction quickly gave way to the reality that whatever was about to happen was going to happen soon. The small black dot was becoming larger much faster than the star behind it, and soon it became more obvious that it was a planet. Somewhere down on the surface Alien-Bot was probably watching us at that very moment and waiting for us to arrive.

"I guess Alien-Bot really wanted us to come over and hang out," Brian said. His voice sounded a little more nervous now.

"Do you think he has video games?" I said, hoping that telling a joke would help calm our nerves.

"I'm sure he does," Brian said, "but they're probably pretty weird games that us humans wouldn't understand. I don't think we're going to understand much of what we find here."

"This place looks nothing like our solar system," I said.

"It's pretty sad, really," Brian said. "It looks like it's almost dead, but the Bots are doing their best to keep it alive. The solar systems we just passed through with the dim stars are dying because the universe is still expanding away from them and the dark matter holding them together is being stretched too far and tearing apart. Without dark matter holding everything together, the laws of physics totally break down and regular matter will just disintegrate into their most basic subatomic parts and scatter into the void like dust."

"Like dust in the wind," I said, thinking about that old song that Daddy is always trying to play on his guitar.

"Right, except there's no wind in a void," Brian said. "It's actually more like 'Quantum Particles Randomly Interacting in a Zero Point Energy Field'. Anyway, to keep the dark energy from stretching apart from the pull of the expanding universe, the Bots built something like a giant balloon that they connected to the edge of the nearest area of the universe where the dark matter isn't being stretched too far. It's like right now we are inside a giant balloon connected to a tank of helium, except the 'tank' is the universe and it is keeping the balloon fed with dark matter instead of helium. Inside the balloon, the dark matter isn't being stretched apart, so the regular matter inside of it can hold itself together. Without this 'balloon', the Red Gwot solar system would have been torn apart a long time ago. On top of that, Red Gwot is a dying red giant star, yet they have somehow managed to stop it from expanding and swallowing Alania whole. It is quite amazing what they have done, but the forces of nature are just too great to sustain these efforts indefinitely."

"It sounds like you do understand this place a little," I said.

"I guess," Brian said. "All you really need to know is that this place should have died a long time ago, but it's still here and they are desperately trying to keep it alive."

Alania basically looked like a big round rock floating in space. The surface looked strange, though, with some sections looking shiny and smooth while other sections were dark and rough. There were no signs of oceans or any other water. Surrounding the planet was a red atmosphere that looked similar to the 'balloon' surrounding the solar system, except this was a perfectly round bubble.

"Is that atmosphere real?" I asked Brian.

"Not the red laser shield," Brian said. "They probably built that after Red-Gwot started expanding to save whatever was left of the atmosphere and to keep themselves from frying like an egg down on the surface."

Soon we noticed something on the surface of the atmosphere that looked like a pair of elevator doors. As we approached, the doors slowly started sliding open as if our arrival was expected. They made no noise as they opened. The only thing I heard was Red-Gwot burning its fuel, which sounded like the distant flames of a wildfire that was getting a little too close for comfort.

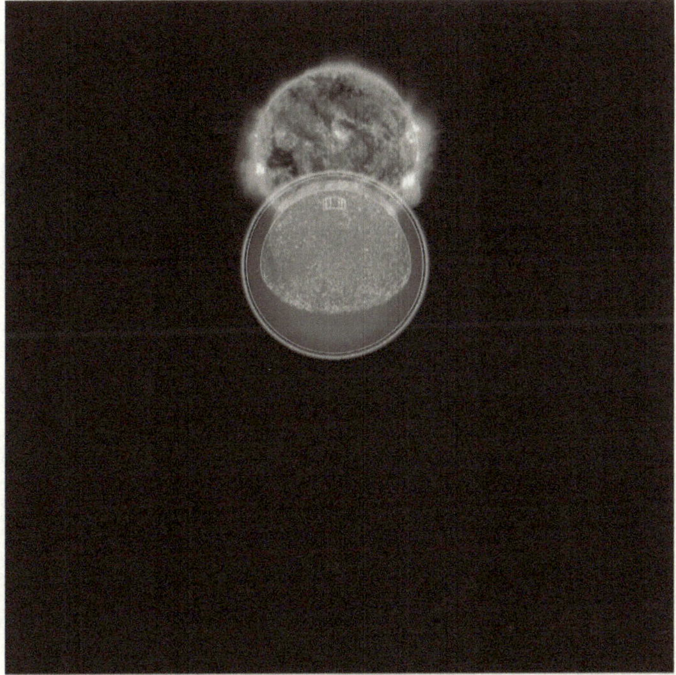

Slowly we descended towards the open doors. At this point I was well beyond fear and now just felt numb. After passing through the doors, they silently started closing above us.

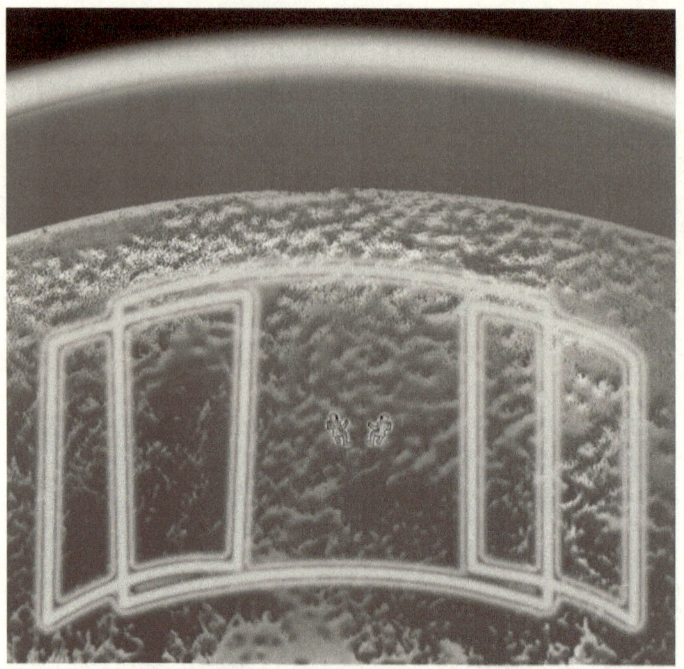

When the doors had closed all the way, the sound of the solar flames vanished into total silence. For the whole journey it almost didn't feel like we were actually moving, but the little jolt I felt when we finally stopped made it obvious that we really had been.

We were now in some kind of huge room with walls made of the same red laser material as the atmosphere shield. Below us another pair of doors started sliding open to reveal a clear view of the scorched surface of the planet.

"We're in some kind of airlock chamber like they have on space vessels," Brian said. "This allows things to come inside without letting the atmosphere out."

When the interior doors were fully open, we slowly started descending. Once inside the main atmosphere, the doors started sliding closed above us. Down on the surface there were what appeared to be charred black rocks surrounded by a smooth shiny surface. A little further down we could see that the rocks were actually small mountains.

We also began to see what looked like paint splotches of all different colors. As we got closer we could see that the splotches weren't flat like paint but instead looked like lumps of melted candle wax. There were no

trees, but there were dot-shaped rocks everywhere that looked like they may have been the remains of trees that had been scorched down to their stumps. Up ahead we saw some larger splotches clustered together, which may have at one time been a great city but was now reduced to the multicolored mix of a molten metropolis.

"I think those smaller splotches are melted houses and the bigger ones are buildings," Brian said. "It looks like this whole planet got toasted. I don't know how anyone could still be living here, and I don't know why they would want to. This place shouldn't even exist."

"Why wouldn't they just go live somewhere else?" I asked.

"I don't know," Brian said. "I guess because this is their home and they don't want to leave. I certainly know what it feels like to lose my home. When Mom and I moved out of our house in East Plains, that was one of the worst experiences of my life. The only thing worse is never having met my father."

"Maybe someday you'll find him," I said.

"Maybe," Brian said.

Up ahead of us a blue light appeared on the horizon. As we got closer we saw that it was a dome down on the surface that looked similar in material to the red atmosphere shield surrounding the planet. Inside the glowing blue dome there appeared to be a small city with some tall buildings surrounded by a bunch of smaller structures.

Upon arriving at the dome we passed through another airlock chamber. When we were all the way inside, a message appeared on my cyborg screen:

ATMOSHPERIC CONDITIONS SUITABLE FOR CYBORG-HUMANS

Suddenly our fire armor retracted and we were now floating above the buildings in the clothes we had worn to school. The temperature was very comfortable and felt like walking into an air conditioned house on a hot summer day.

The city looked like it had just been built, but no one seemed to be living there. There were about ten or so skyscrapers that looked similar in shape to the newer towers of Manhattan, but these were built with shiny metal of very bright colors such as red, blue, green, and purple. In fact, everything in the city seemed to be made of metal. The streets were shiny gold and the sidewalks were shiny silver. Glittering metallic trees and plants of all different colors lined the sidewalks and filled small parks, but it didn't look like there were any actual living plants. A couple of the parks had ponds and streams that were the light blue color of swimming pools. It was a strange and beautiful place, but the fact that it was completely deserted made it feel very creepy.

Just outside of downtown we floated over a neighborhood of metal houses that also looked brand new and empty. Beyond that was a large hill, the surface of which was a nicely landscaped version of the scorched ground outside the blue dome.

And, on top of the hill, a ginormous white mansion surrounded by a huge field of blue grass overlooked the city. Behind the mansion sat another large building with an enormous observatory dome on top of it. The entire property was surrounded by a red laser wall that must have been a hundred feet high.

"I bet I know who lives there," Brian said.

I heard Brian's voice in my helmet, but I was becoming so distracted by the bright red glow of the fence that I was unable to respond. As we got closer the glow began to hurt my eyes, and soon everything around us started turning red. Eventually it became so blinding that I had to close my eyes.

The next thing I knew I was lying sideways on the floor of a brightly lit white room. I tried to move but I couldn't because my arms were tied behind my back and my ankles were bound with red laser handcuffs. It took a minute for my eyes to adjust to the brightness, but after they did I saw Brian unconscious on the floor next to me. Like me he was on his side bound with red laser handcuffs at the ankles and at the wrists behind his back. I tried to move again and managed to wiggle just enough to notice that in one corner of the room there was a door with red laser bars.

Moments later Brian made a grunting noise. He then opened his eyes but started squinting because of the bright light.

"Where are we?" he asked.

"I think we're in Alien-Bot's jail," I said.

"That is correct, *human cyborgs,*" said an electronic voice from somewhere in the room. It sounded like a robot voice except that it wasn't your typical robot monotone. This voice sounded *alive*.

Brian motioned with his head so I would notice the monitor up on the wall. It had a black screen and a white 16-bit pixel face on it.

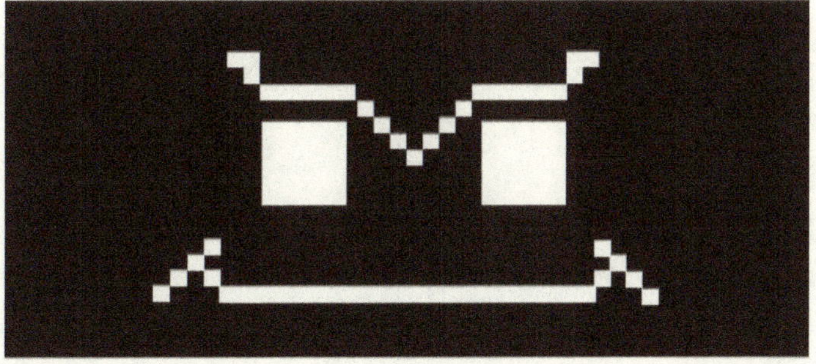

"As I am sure you are already aware, I am Alien-Bot," the voice said, the mouth on the monitor moving as he spoke. "You are inside my home on the planet Alania, which you should now begin to think of as your new home world as well since you will never be leaving here again."

CHAPTER 8

"I apologize for not personally appearing before you," Alien-Bot continued, "but my scans indicated that your transformation bones have been awakened and fitted with some type of custom software that I did not design. I take it that you have been to see that half-wit hacker Sven, and that he is responsible for these low-tech upgrades. But no matter. I am working on a cloaking device that will allow me to personally appear before you so that you will not be able to scan me and transform into my profile. My scans also detected that my meteor rays did not fully install my controller interface into your cyborg systems. Again, a simple fix that I am working on. Your systems will be updated shortly and at that time you will no longer be the masters of your own thoughts."

"You can't do this!" I said angrily, but as soon as the words were out I realized that I needed to stay calm.

"Oh yes I can," Alien-Bot said. The white pixel face seemed to be grinning wickedly.

"Why did you bring us here?" I asked calmly.

"So you can help me restore Alania to its former glory," Alien-Bot said. "And the first step in that process is to destroy the universe."

"So you want to make Alania great again by destroying the universe?" Brian asked with the same grin he had whenever he questioned Mayor Martinez about one of her policies that he didn't agree with.

"Precisely," Alien-Bot said.

"But why do you have to destroy the universe to do this?" I asked.

"I have traveled all over the universe," Alien-Bot said, "and have discovered that most civilizations are ruled by criminals, fools, thieves, murderers, liars, and cheats. Everything they have accomplished they owe to the Alanian civilization, which was the spawning point of all the intelligent life that followed in this universe. Yet they show no gratitude, nor do they acknowledge our importance to their own accomplishments. They are content to let our world die while they reap the rewards of our greatness. But this Alanian carnage stops right here and right now. From this moment on, it will be Alania first. We will take back the resources that their galaxies have thrived on and use them to rebuild our own civilization. Alania will start winning again, winning like never before. We will build new cities. We will bring back our wealth. We will bring back our dreams. And we will eradicate completely the rest of the universe so that our enemies will no longer be able to take advantage of our greatness."

"Oh, *now* I get it," Brian said, this time sounding serious but I could tell he was being sarcastic. "You want to drain the universe first *and then* destroy it. Now it all makes sense."

"I am relieved to hear that you approve," Alien-Bot said. "And I am sure that all of my other cyborgs will approve as well without the insolence you are presently displaying. That is because their minds are already under my control, just as yours will be as soon as I finish this patch that I will be uploading to your cyborg systems."

"There are more like us?" I asked.

"Of course," Alien-Bot said. "They are

traveling here from all over the universe at this very moment and will begin arriving shortly. Since my own people have made the foolish decision to go elsewhere to fulfill their selfish needs instead of staying home and fixing the problems here, I need to repopulate Alania with the best and brightest minds that the universe has to offer. The fleeing cowards who were unwilling to fight to save their home world deserve to perish with the rest of the ungrateful universe. The two of you should consider yourselves fortunate to have been chosen among the select few who will not only be spared, but also to have the opportunity to be part of the great new society I am building."

"That's a pretty stupid plan for someone who's supposed to be the smartest scientist in the universe," Brian said.

Alien-Bot did not respond, and I started to feel uncomfortable like I did when Brian spoke to Mayor Martinez like this because I could tell it really annoyed her. My instincts were telling me that Brian was making a poor decision here and that I needed to change the subject before he said something that would make our situation even worse.

"Why did you choose us?" I asked.

"Because the human mind has the potential

to achieve super-intelligence," Alien-Bot said. "I often find this difficult to believe considering how your people conduct themselves, but the science backs up my theory. Your brains have the potential, but you have yet to tap into it— although I am getting some unexpected activity readings from the brain of the red one here."

"But why *us*?" I asked. "Why me and him?"

"Because the two of you are on the hyperactive wavelength," Alien-Bot said. "Organic beings on the hyperactive wavelength generally have the most intelligent, most creative, most productive minds in the universe. The meteors were programmed to first identify humans on this wavelength, then search for more specific characteristics. These characteristics are classified by color. Once the more specific characteristics were identified, the meteors beamed the different colored cyborg conversion rays. Obviously, you, green one, were identified as having an inquisitive scientific mind and strong analytical instincts, so you were beamed with green conversion rays. As for you, red one, you were identified as having the ability to intimidate others and plow through assigned tasks without letting their potential objections become a distraction.

My data analysis also indicated that you have the potential to be extremely loyal to one who acts as the father figure you never had, which would, of course, be me, the father of this new generation of Bots."

"You'll never be a father figure to me!" Brian yelled, his nostrils flaring like the old BullBorg.

"There is a perfect example of the red classification," Alien-Bot said. "As for the loyalty part, that will fall into place after I assume control of your minds. But I am still puzzled as to what happened to the pink one."

"The *pink* one?" I asked.

"Yes," Alien-Bot said. "There were supposed to be three of you from Earth."

"What does the pink classification mean?" I asked.

"Those are the females," Alien-Bot said. "Bots are still part organic, and therefore we still need females to keep the species alive."

"Is having children the only thing you think females are good for?" Brian asked, his nostrils flaring again. "You sick monster!"

I knew I had to cut him off immediately.

"The universe is not trying to destroy Alania," I said calmly. "You are the most intelligent being in the universe and the greatest scientist ever. That's why you must know that Red-Gwot and Alania aren't dying because someone or something is trying to destroy it. It is simply the nature of this universe. Things are born, they live, and they die when they get too old."

"And you don't have to stay here," Brian said calmly, his nostrils no longer flaring. I was relieved that he had followed my lead. "There are plenty of other places to live. You don't have to stay here and try to save this place. All great civilizations eventually come to an end. And now you can build a newer and better civilization for the Bots in a place that will last billions of more years without constantly struggling to keep this place alive. Maybe then your people will join you and help. They just didn't want to stay here because this place is dying, and they didn't want to die with it."

"Silence!" Alien-Bot said. "Alania is a sacred planet that is more important than all the planets in the universe combined. In short order, Alania and Red-Gwot *will* be the universe. Now I must finish preparing your mind control patches and then finish preparing this solar system to survive without being tethered to the rest of the universe. Meanwhile, I suggest you reconsider your good fortune of being among the chosen few who will be part of my empire!"

Suddenly the face on the monitor disappeared and the screen turned as white as the walls around it so that it was no longer visible. Brian then looked at me and I looked back at him and saw that his eyes were now open extra wide and turning bright blue like Sven's. The look on his face became uncomfortable to the point where I wanted to turn away, but when I tried to I couldn't. His eyes wouldn't let me!

The room was totally silent until I thought I heard someone calling my name. At first I could barely hear it, but then I heard it again and this time it was a little louder and clearer. When I heard it a third time I realized that it was Brian's voice, but I didn't know where it was coming from since he was right in front of me and his lips were not moving. Eventually I realized that the voice was inside my mind — he was communicating with me telepathically! I then stopped trying to fight the impulse to look away from his eyes, and after that my mind was able to hear him loud and clear.

"Don't say anything," Brian's voice said, "and don't send any messages. Alien-Bot can monitor our cyborg systems, but he can't read our human minds. Just stay focused on my voice. If you have any transformation scans on your drive, blink once. If not, blink twice."

I blinked once.

"Blink once if what you scanned is large, blink twice if it is small."

Ralston was the only scan I had, so I blinked twice.

"Blink once if you think it can fit through the bars on the door, blink twice if not."

It was hard to tell if Ralston could fit through the laser bars. Ralston may have been a fat old cat, but I had seen him squeeze through some narrow spaces in search of a good spot to take a nap. He was able to make himself surprisingly narrow by stretching his legs and back as much as possible, so I blinked once to let Brian know that I thought I could.

"Good," Brian's voice said. "My scan file is a small thing too, so on the count of three, transform into it. That should make our hands and legs small enough to slip out of these handcuffs. Then we need to squeeze through the bars and make a run for it. We won't have much time because Alien-Bot will know we escaped and he'll be tracking us. So, get ready to transform on three. One.. two… three!"

I successfully transformed into Ralston and easily stepped out of the laser cuffs that were now on the floor around my paws. But when I saw Brian, I stopped for a moment in pure shock at what I was seeing. Brian had transformed into a cyborg chicken!

Brian clucked at me and ran towards the door. He was a little wider than me but was able to squeeze through one of the openings between the laser bars, although a few of his feathers got zapped on the way out. I followed him through the same opening by doing Ralston's stretching trick and made it through without any of my fur getting zapped. On the other side of the door we then transformed back into our human forms.

"This way!" Brian said. We started running down a long hallway, and moments later the lights started flashing and a very loud alarm started going off. We eventually reached the end of the hallway and arrived at another one where we had to decide to turn right or left. We stopped and looked both ways, but each direction looked the same. I was about to tell Brian to just pick one when a hologram of what looked like Alien-Bot appeared before us, except his armor wasn't shiny and it had lots of dents and scratches. The red lights of his eyes also looked dim, and his tentacles were hanging lifelessly down his back to the floor. He looked very old and tired.

I thought we were done for, but the Bot said, "I am a friend. A portal is about to open. Run through it to reach safety." His voice was soft and calm, and while it was electronic like Alien-Bot's, it sounded less robotic and more organic. A circular portal then opened to our right that was just big enough for each of us to pass through one at a time. Unlike the blue lightning of the wormhole, this one had a glowing neon green border.

I was ready to follow Brian through, but he didn't move.

"Go!" I said.

"How do we know we can trust him?" Brian asked.

"We can!" I said. "My instincts are telling me we can!"

I guess that was good enough for Brian because he stepped into the portal and disappeared, and I quickly followed. Suddenly everything turned blindingly bright, but a moment later we found ourselves standing in a valley of shiny silver dirt surrounded by black mountains and a couple of colorful splotches of melted houses nearby. It was very hot and it was difficult to breathe. The big red sun was setting on the horizon before us. The hologram and the portal were nowhere to be seen.

"Where are we?" I asked.

"We're still on Alania, but we seem to be outside the blue dome," Brian said.

Suddenly another portal appeared about ten feet away.

"Deploy fire armor and activate fire blaster!" Brian commanded. I repeated his command, and in a matter of seconds we were both covered in our armor and aiming our blasters at the portal.

"Be ready to use the power bomb," Brian said.

"Please power down," said a voice that I recognized as the one belonging to the hologram. But the hologram was nowhere in sight, and the voice sounded like it was coming from inside the portal.

"Power down!" I said, and my blaster retracted. Brian looked at me and I nodded, but it still took him a while to finally decide it was safe to power down.

The old bot we had earlier seen as a hologram now appeared for real at the entrance of the portal—but he did not step through it to where we were. And this portal looked different than the other one, as there was no border around it and the edge was blurry and blended into the background. Behind the old bot was not darkness but a moving orange glow as if a fire was burning somewhere behind him.

"Step into this portal," the old bot said. "This location will be discovered very soon, but the portal is undetectable and leads to a hiding place that no one can find. You will be safe here."

"Who are you?" Brian asked.

"I am Gor-Bot," he answered. "I am the only one who can help you in this world. I am the father of the one you know as 'Alien-Bot'."

CHAPTER 9

This time there was no blinding light as we passed through the portal, and we immediately emerged on the other side as if we had just stepped into another room. The portal then silently closed behind us like an expanding ripple on a pond of still water.

We found ourselves standing in a ginormous cavern with a flowing lava river that had numerous lava falls feeding into it. The glow of the lava made the cavern surprisingly bright and gave the dark ground and rocky walls an orange glow. It was mostly quiet except for the gentle boiling bubble sounds echoing against the walls.

The message about acceptable atmospheric conditions for cyborg-humans appeared on our cyborg screens, but this time it asked if we wanted to retract our armor. I retracted mine first, then a moment later Brian did the same. The air was hot, but not as hot as it had been outside, and it was much easier to breathe.

Gor-Bot was standing off to the side as if allowing us take in the amazing view in front of us. Eventually he said, "I hope you feel comfortable and are having no difficulty breathing. Us Bots have similar biological requirements as humans, as do most intelligent beings throughout the universe. The radiation levels are also acceptable down here, unlike the high levels up on the surface."

"Where are we?" I asked.

"We are deep beneath the surface of Alania," Gor-Bot said. "This is actually an old hiding spot of mine that I have never told anyone about until now, including my son. This cavern serves as a natural protection against the elements, and I designed a cloaking device that further conceals it. I used to conduct experiments in a laboratory that I built down here. These experiments were not approved by the Alanian government of the time, so I had to work in secret. I was trying to find a way to permanently stop Red-Gwot from expanding, which I thought was a good thing, but my work was considered too dangerous. And it was dangerous, but I was determined. I worked on this until my son was born. That event changed my perspective on what matters most, so I stopped the work. Anyway, we have much to discuss. First let us go down to the ship and get comfortable."

We followed Gor-Bot on a narrow footpath that ran along the lava river until we reached a Viking ship that looked like the one from the painting in Sven's office. A little further down the river there was a small rectangular building that looked like it was carved out of magmatic rock. Gor-Bot stopped in front of the old ship and turned to us.

"This ship is from your home world," he said. "And the building over there is my laboratory."

"The *Universal Explorer*!" I said. "This is Sven's old ship! You must be the friend he was talking about who taught him all that stuff!"

"Precisely," Gor-Bot said. "This is a special vessel. Even with all of our technology, us Bots would never have been able to build a ship like this. It is truly a work of art from another world. We never had wood like this on Alania, at least not in my lifetime. Sven said that Earth does not even have wood like this anymore. My son and I explored the universe with this ship until he got sick. Now it has been my home for the past ten or so of your Earth years."

We followed Gor-Bot up an old wooden plank that was being used as a boarding ramp to the ship's main deck. The ship looked much bigger from here than it did from the outside, though it was still nowhere near the size of huge modern ships. The interior was decorated more like a modern house than an old Viking ship. Only the old wooden table and benches in the middle of the deck looked like they came from the era when the ship was built. The lighting fixtures, shelves, end tables, and most of the other furniture looked like they came from that big furniture store where you can buy Swedish meatballs and bookcases that you have to put together like a Blockos set when you get home. There was a modern kitchen, a modern bathroom, and a huge flatscreen television that showed live images of various places on Alania—including Alien-Bot's house. The only alien-looking things were the weird couches lined against the walls that looked like they were made from Jel-EEE dessert gelatin of all different colors.

Gor-Bot invited us to have a seat on the couches, and I didn't notice until we were seated that Brian was sitting on a red Jel-EEE couch and I was sitting on a green one. Although it was a little wobbly, the couch was comfortable and suddenly made me realize how tired I was. Brian looked tired as well.

"I apologize if the accommodations are not suitable," Gor-Bot said. "I am not accustomed to having guests."

"No, this is really cool," Brian said. "I wish my house was this nice."

"I have always felt guilty about possessing this ship because I know how much it means to my dear friend Sven," Gor-Bot said. "But I did not realize this back when we made our deal.

That was a long time ago now. At the time he said that he was ready to stop exploring the seas of Earth and start doing something new, but he needed the knowledge I possessed to get started. So together we converted this ship into a space vessel, which is how I taught him the technology. It seemed like a fair deal at the time, and I think it has worked out well for the both of us. In better times my son and I explored many galaxies with this ship, and I know I probably would not have been able to survive the last ten years without it."

"How did you first meet Sven?" I asked.

"I first encountered Sven on Earth many of your centuries ago, long before my son was born," Gor-Bot said. "I was doing some space exploration on my own in a small research vessel I had built myself. I was looking for anything that might help with my work to save Red-Gwot when I came across your sun, which is a yellow dwarf much like Red-Gwot had been before it started running out of fuel and became a red giant—in fact, our distant ancestors had actually called our sun 'Yellow-Gwot'. However, as I got closer to your sun, I started pickup up some unusual readings coming from the oceans of Earth. These readings were coming from the creatures you know as 'krakens', so I descended to the surface to investigate and found that one of them was attacking this very ship.

"I realized that what I was about to do was possibly a violation of the Universal Space Code regarding native species, as it is against the law to interfere with the affairs of native species on their home planet. But there was something odd about these kraken creatures, and I suspected that they themselves were not native to Earth and were actually aliens who were already interfering. My instincts told me that I should help Sven and his crew because if the krakens were alien to Earth, then I would be legally permitted to help.

"So I used my sonar blaster to scare the kraken away, and the ship was spared without any damage or injuries to the crew. But the presence of my vessel frightened Sven's crew even more than the kraken had. I understood this and was ready to leave, but Sven was not afraid and signaled for me to stay. He knew that I had helped them, and he was not afraid of me just because I was different. We have been friends ever since.

"Sven's people were great explorers on Earth long before the rest of humankind caught up to them. I understood this well because my people, the Bots, were also explorers. But navigating the oceans of Earth was a hard life, and over time Sven said some of his people became disillusioned by the concept of exploring and became what he called 'raiders'. These raiders would travel to distant shores and attack the native population and take everything of value. The attacks were so violent that the victims wouldn't even consider seeking revenge.

"The collective mind of Sven's people eventually became poisoned with greed. Those who were not 'explorers' did not witness the violence of raiding and pillaging innocent people, and the wealth they were accumulating made them deaf to the tales of horror associated with it. Sven tried to make them understand, but those who had benefitted most from these raids began to see him as a threat. Sven soon realized that the more he tried to convince them the error of their ways, the more dangerous they became to him. He then discovered a plot by his own crew to murder him and take over his ship, so he devised a plan to trick them by telling them he would allow them to raid a wealthy village he knew about and keep the spoils all to themselves. They sailed to an uncharted island that only

Sven knew was uninhabited and told his crew that the villagers were so wealthy that they lived hidden in the middle of the forest so that their riches could not be seen from the shore. He dropped anchor just offshore and watched from the ship as his crew rowed to the beach and disappeared into the forest. Their minds were so infected with greed that they did not consider the possibility that they were being tricked. As soon as they had disappeared into the trees, Sven pulled the anchor and set sail across the Atlantic Ocean to begin his new life.

"The *Universal Explorer* was faster than any other Viking ship, so no one would be able to catch him. On the other side of the ocean he landed on the shores of what is now known as Oak Island in the country that you now know as Canada. He hid his ship in a swamp that was not visible offshore and buried the treasures that he and his crew had legitimately collected over the years. He set up numerous booby traps for anyone who might happen to find him on the island and start looking for the treasure. He built himself a house and settled in, but then he didn't know what to do with himself. He was still a relatively young man, and he felt that there was a lot he could still accomplish in his life.

"It was at this point where I returned to Earth and located his ship on Oak Island. I landed my vessel in the swamp there and was greeted warmly by Sven, who seemed very lonely and depressed. He said he was looking for a new adventure, and when I invited him to inspect my own little ship, he was fascinated and said he wanted to learn about our Bot technology. I told him I was thinking of building a new larger space vessel, and Sven made a joke saying that he had an old ship he needed to get rid of but that it was only good for the oceans of Earth. I was fascinated with his ship and suggested I could convert it into a space vessel, and he was fascinated by the technology behind my little ship. So we made a deal to trade ships, and I taught him about Bot technology by having him help me convert the *Universal Explorer* into a space vessel. I could tell that he did love his old ship, but he thought it would actually be safer with me because he was worried that it might be discovered in the swamp by Viking raiders and used for raiding, or perhaps even destroyed as an act of revenge. He also liked the idea that the *Universal Explorer* would actually be used to explore the universe, and he said my ship would be a new toy for him to play with.

"I taught him what I knew through the process of converting the *Universal Explorer* into a space vessel. I also taught him how to use some of our other technology to prolong his life. This life extending technology is ancient to us Bots and is how our people became cyborgs. We were once totally organic beings, but we eventually discovered this technology and it changed everything for us. Over billions of years our mechanical parts evolved and became caretakers for our organic hearts and brains, which has allowed us to live for very long periods of time. Your people on Earth are actually now at the beginning of this same process of technological discovery and potential evolution."

"Does that mean that Sven turned himself into a cyborg?" I asked.

"Yes, but not exactly like the two of you," Gor-Bot said. "The cyborg technology that you now possess came directly from us Bots, thanks to my son. Sven took the technology I taught him and created his own version of it. So, technically he is a cyborg, but his technology is different than yours and mine.

"When the work was completed, I invited Sven to join me in my travels, but he said he had work left to do on Earth. He was determined to convince his people that raiding was wrong and was willing to use the technology I had taught him to scare them into realizing this. He also wanted to help vulnerable people learn how to defend themselves against raiders.

"So I took the ship back to Alania and hid it down here in this cavern, where I continued to tinker with it. This ship became my new passion, and my ultimate goal was to use it to explore the universe in search of scientific knowledge that would help me save Red-Gwot. At the same time I would also be looking for uninhabited planets that could be a suitable home for my people if we reached the point where we had to evacuate.

"During this time, I got married and my wife gave birth to our son. Unfortunately, there were complications during childbirth and my wife died shortly afterwards. You know my son as 'Alien-Bot', but my wife and I had named him 'Sci-Bot' because we both shared a love of science. Sci-Bot was a good child, and he is still one of the greatest scientific minds in the entire universe. And I know that the goodness is still inside of him, but it has been suppressed by the sickness he has suffered.

"After he had graduated from the science

university, I completed his education by teaching him almost everything I knew. I say 'almost' because there are still a few things I know that he does not. We then set out on our quest in the newly retrofitted *Universal Explorer*. These were glorious times for me, the happiest days of my life. We explored many galaxies and encountered many welcoming civilizations. But we also encountered societies who are mistrustful of outsiders, and even though we would clearly state that we were on a peaceful mission to acquire scientific knowledge, they would perceive our presence as a threat. Some civilizations do not believe that scientific knowledge and modern technology are necessarily good things. Although I do not agree with these societies, they have every right to possess their own beliefs, and I have no right to attempt to force my own beliefs on them.

"And then there are those societies whose leaders do not believe in freedom at all and will actually attack anyone—including their own citizens—who do not share their established beliefs. As disturbing as it is to encounter a society that denies its citizens even the most basic freedoms of thought and speech, there is little that an outsider—

especially two scientists in an old Viking ship—can do.

"We encountered such a society on a planet named Kidok in the Tiran Galaxy. As we neared this world we sent our usual peaceful greeting, and we were surprised when we received two separate responses. The first one came on the main messaging frequency from the Kidokian government ordering us to leave the solar system immediately or else they would attack. The second one was a mysterious signal that Sci-Bot picked up outside the standard messaging frequency range. He locked onto the signal and decoded a message asking us to help because they were in great danger. Their star was about to go supernova, but their leaders were in denial of this and were persecuting anyone who disagreed with them. We did some quick scans and it was quite obvious that their star really was about to go supernova. It would surely destroy their planet and everything else near it. They would all die, and all that would remain of their solar system would be a black hole.

"So we hailed the government channel and informed them of our readings. We were quite surprised when they responded that there was nothing wrong with their star and that fake news was being spread by a small group of rogue activists and dishonest news media. This was startling. Even an amateur scientist could tell that the star was about to go supernova. We responded by showing them evidence that was undeniable, but the more proof we presented, the angrier they became. They called us 'evil aliens' who were threatening to destroy their way of life. They pointed weapons at our ship and warned us that they would not hesitate to use them.

"My instincts told me that the general population of Kidok was being held hostage by their leaders, who likely saw us as a threat to their wealth and power. This is a play that has been acted out repeatedly throughout the history of our universe, including on your own planet. Dictators such as this will do anything to hold on to their wealth and power—even if it means the destruction of everything and everyone. Their minds are so diseased that it is not possible to reason with them. The only way their ignorance and arrogance can be stopped is through a revolution by the people.

"I told Sci-Bot that there was nothing more we could do and that we had to leave. This was difficult for him to accept. I had seen things like this before so I was able to accept it.

But Sci-Bot was young and had not encountered evil such as this, so his mind struggled to accept the reality of it. It also truly angered him that he was only trying to help them and do what most would consider the right thing to do, yet he was called an 'evil alien' for his efforts.

"In one last desperate effort, Sci-Bot sent out a message to the entire population over an unencrypted open channel with instructions about how to create local wormholes that would lead them to the moon of a class M planet we had discovered where they would be safe. It is never a good idea to send out an unencrypted message over an open channel, especially to so many people at once, because it leaves you exposed to responses that can contain viruses. The government responded to him with a message of their own warning us never to return to their solar system, then fired a laser missile at us that fortunately missed.

"After we had left the Kidokian system, I tried to get him to focus on continuing our mission so we could help our own cause. I also reminded him that there were many others in the universe who could use our help and would gratefully accept it. There were times when I thought I was getting through to him, but it soon became clear that something was not right with his mind. He was becoming less responsive to me and had started making very obvious technical errors. But every time I asked him if something was wrong, he became very angry and insisted that he was fine and demanded that I stop asking him that.

"It wasn't long after our encounter with the Kidokians that their sun did go supernova. We went back to inspect it, but we couldn't get anywhere near it because of the black hole that was now there. The Kidokians were gone, and there was no evidence that they were ever there except for a brief entry in the Universal Database.

"Of course I felt devastated that we couldn't help the Kidokian people. I thought that Sci-Bot would be upset as well, but he showed no emotion whatsoever and suggested we return to Alania immediately. From then on it felt like my son wasn't really there even when he was sitting right beside me.

"On our way home I continued to identify uninhabited planets as potential sites for the relocation of our own people who had not yet fled Alania, but Sci-Bot did not participate. I had not been able to discover a way to stop Red-Gwot from expanding, and knowing that it would soon expand to the point where the atmosphere of Alania would start burning off and all life on the planet would begin to die, my plan was to present my list of suitable planets to our people and we could then together decide which one of them to make our new home.

"Upon our return, however, we discovered that Alania's atmosphere was deteriorating at a much faster rate than it had been when we left. Most of the remaining population was already gone, though there were still a few holdouts attempting to build a shield around the planet to contain the atmosphere. They thought the shield would buy them more time to figure out a way to stop Red-Gwot from expanding. This shield would be similar to the one built by our ancestors around our solar system when our part of the universe began to die millions of years ago. The dark matter that holds the universe together had begun spreading too thin in our galaxy because the rest of the universe in front of us was continually expanding at an increasing rate. In other words, we are at the very end of the line and the rest of the universe is pulling away from us, and our old galaxy couldn't keep up the pace and was literally being stretched and torn apart. The shield they built around the solar system managed to hold a pocket of dark matter together in something like a big bag that they connected to the rest of the universe by the tube you traveled through to get here. It was an ingenious design that allowed this place to survive much longer than it would have without it, as the bag managed to hold the dark matter together while the bag itself was being towed along by rest of the universe as it expanded. Yet nothing in this universe can last forever, nor is the universe itself immortal.

"Sci-Bot and I inspected the work they had been doing on the new atmosphere shield. I concluded that they would not be able to get it working in time and that the atmosphere was going to deteriorate beyond repair very soon. The scientists accepted my assessment and finally decided to leave, but then Sci-Bot came back to them and said that he had not only discovered a way to make the shield work in time, he had also discovered a way to stop Red-Gwot from expanding.

"This was very surprising to me because I surely thought he would agree with the plan to evacuate. Even if he had found a way to stop Red-Gwot from expanding, there would be no one or nothing left to save. Most of the people were already gone and the surface of the planet would be in ruins by the time it was finished. It was also very troubling that he refused to reveal his plan to me or the other scientists. He just kept talking about how he was going to restore Alania to its former glory and fix all the problems that the previous generations had caused. It all sounded like nonsense to me and I thought for sure that his unrealistic promises and arrogant boasting would be a warning sign to the scientists, but they enthusiastically believed everything he said and decided to stay and work with him.

"I was stunned. Their decision went against all the norms of scientific analysis and reason. It was simply not logical. It was obvious to me that Sci-Bot's sickness was causing him to mislead them, and that his enthusiasm towards restoring Alania to greatness was blinding their judgment.

"So I privately met with the scientists and told them that I thought my son was not mentally fit to fulfill the promises he had made. But they said they trusted him more than they trusted me because Sci-Bot was the best scientist in the universe, and I was part of the old establishment who had allowed the solar system to reach the point of destruction in the first place. It almost seemed as if they believed him simply because they wanted to, even though the hard science was clearly pointing towards disaster.

"At first they were happy to have a great scientist like Sci-Bot helping them, but this did not last long. They quickly realized that something was not right with his mind. Sci-Bot did actually manage to get the shield working and also temporarily stop Red-Gwot from expanding, but the scientists had come to fear him because he would attack anyone who disagreed with him regardless of whether they were right or wrong. Loyalty was the only thing that mattered to him, but his treatment of them caused them all to turn against him. Behind his back they referred to him as 'Mad-Bot' and 'Psycho-Bot', and eventually they fled Alania fearing for their lives.

"Being abandoned by the scientists made Sci-Bot even more defiant. He became angry at the entire universe and felt like he had been alienated by everyone he had ever known except for me. This is when he started referring to himself as 'Alien-Bot'. He vowed to save Alania and restore our civilization at any cost.

"I remained close to him and pretended to be on his side. This gave me the chance to hack into his database, where I found two sets of plans he had drawn up that would stop Red-Gwot from expanding by giving it a new energy source.

"The first plan involved infusing a living organic energy source into the core of Red-Gwot once a year. This essentially meant that someone who was wholly or partially organic—someone like you or I—would have to be fed alive to Red-Gwot once a year. Just the fact that he would even consider such a horrific plan showed the depth of his sickness.

"Yet the second plan was even worse. This one involved recharging the core of Red Gwot with scattered organic energy from the main part of the universe. When organic beings die, their leftover energy scatters and eventually gets absorbed by the universe. The only way to harness this energy would be to tear a hole in the space-time continuum and use a large hose to pump the organic energy that spilled out of it directly into the heart of Red-Gwot. The hose itself would pass through the tube connecting our solar system to the main part of the universe. This would be a one-time permanent fix for our sun, but the hole in the space-time continuum would be irreparable and continue to grow larger and larger at a faster rate. The main part of the universe would quickly start to collapse onto itself before anyone could do anything about it. After Red-Gwot received the energy it needed, the hose and the tube could simply be disconnected and the solar system container sealed off so that we would no longer be connected to the rest of the universe.

"Red-Gwot would be more powerful than ever. It would be able to fuel itself and the solar system container holding the dark matter in place for billions of years. Our solar system would essentially exist as a tiny universe inside a bubble floating through the void with a prime view of the main universe suffering a horrible death.

"Now that the scientists were gone, I was the only one left who could try to talk some sense into my son. I thought that he might at least consider what I had to say because I am his father, but I knew I had to wait for the right moment. When it finally came, I told him of how his mother and I once spoke of moving away from Alania to a place where we would be able to do science that could benefit the entire universe without the constant distraction of trying to save a world that was going to eventually die anyway no matter how hard we tried to save it. We would invite all Alanians to join us and keep our civilization and cultural traditions alive. It wouldn't matter what planet we were on or what galaxy we were in. What had made our civilization great in the first place was our people, and it could thrive indefinitely as long as we were together.

"For a brief moment I saw a sparkle in his eyes, but that quickly disappeared and he went back to work without responding. I knew I had failed, so I desperately began to appeal to his sense of logic. I told him that I had located a relatively young star with a planet in its orbit that was larger and more dynamic than ours had ever been where we could build a bigger, better version of our civilization. I reminded him that our people were already gone and did not wish to return, so he would not be able to rebuild our civilization here even if he did fix Red-Gwot. We were the only ones left, so the decision to carry on was now ours alone. It would be much simpler to start rebuilding our civilization elsewhere. At this point there was no reason to save Alania, and it was cruel to continue trying to do so because it was clearly suffering. Alania could never return to its former beauty. Besides, all living things eventually had to die, including the stars and the planets and the universe itself. It was not our place to disrupt the natural order when there was no valid reason to do so. And trying to save Alania would probably do more harm to the legacy of our civilization than if we simply allowed our beloved planet to die a peaceful, dignified death of its own accord. This would bring closure and remove the uncertainty our people must be feeling about the future of our civilization. Finally we could officially reboot our people's government elsewhere and give them a place they can comfortably call 'home'.

"I thought I had made some sound arguments, but my efforts to reason with him only made it worse. He said I was either with him or against him and that he would kill me if he had to. I didn't think he would ever do anything to harm me, but he was very sick.

"My next plan was to try and capture him. That way I could bring him elsewhere and allow nature to take its course regarding Red-Gwot and Alania. I would then summon the top medical minds in the universe to help him.

"I thought I had found an opening where I could slip past the defense system of his house, but it was a trap. He created the opening himself and was waiting for me when I got there. He said he now knew for sure that I was against him and shot me with his lasers. He left me to die just outside the fence surrounding his house.

"Normally such an attack would have easily killed me, but I was wearing new armor that I built specifically to protect me against his lasers. But I wanted to make sure he thought I was dead, so I transmitted a false signal indicating that I had died and that my self-destruct sequence had been activated. I then opened one of my undetectable portals next to me and set down a power bomb that I programmed to go off in three seconds. I quickly rolled into the portal and closed it just before the bomb went off.

"I must have convinced him that I was dead because I have been hiding down here monitoring his actions ever since and he hasn't done anything to indicate that he is looking for me. I have also been attempting to subtly sabotage his efforts so that he wouldn't notice that someone was working against him, but that has been difficult. He used thousands of robotic construction workers to build his new city, which is presumably where the cyborgs he is summoning to populate his new civilization will live. I also overheard him say to the two of you that he intends to destroy the universe, which means he is likely working on the second of his plans to repair Red-Gwot—the one where he will tear a hole in the space-time continuum in the main universe and pump the energy from it into Red-Gwot's core.

"The two of you and the other cyborgs who are on their way now were surely part of those plans, but he was not able to gain control of your two minds. This may be a result of my effort to sabotage the meteors he sent out to convert you and the others into cyborgs. While I was unable to stop him from sending these meteors, I did attempt to infect them with a viral code intended to block him from achieving mind control. I think it worked with your meteors, which were the first ones sent, but the thousands sent afterwards had stronger firewalls built into them. I suspect he noticed that something was wrong with those first ones sent to Earth and corrected the problem for the others. This means that the other cyborgs may not have control of their minds.

"Anyway, you are safe here at the moment, but he is surely searching for you and has probably realized by now that someone is helping you. I have set up various decoys with your cyborg signatures to make it look like you are presently traveling through a series of known portals up on the surface, but he is too smart to deceive for long and it is only a matter of time before he discovers my deception."

Brian and I looked at each other. This was the most unbelievable story I had ever heard, but I was too tired to fully understand it. I just wanted to go home. I started getting that feeling I had before I started crying, but the look on Brian's face stopped me from doing so. He actually looked hopeful.

"I think I know how to destroy him," he said to Gor-Bot.

"No," Gor-Bot said. "He is my son. I cannot destroy him."

"But he tried to kill you!" I said.

"He is my son, and he is sick," Gor-Bot said. "I cannot destroy him. I can only try to help him—and this is where I need the two of you to help me capture him. I would normally never ask innocent others to engage in such a dangerous mission, but this involves your home world too. If we are successful, my son will not be able to move forward with his plans, and I will be able to safely send you and the other cyborgs home. However, if we are not successful, the entire universe—including Earth and everyone living there—will be destroyed."

CHAPTER 10

At some point I fell asleep on the couch and dreamed that I was back at home playing video games with Parker. Everything seemed fine until Parker suddenly stopped playing and looked at me with a strange expression on his face. I thought he was going to say something silly or ask me if he could go in my room to borrow one of my toys, but instead he very calmly asked, "Are you going to save the universe so that we don't die?"

I suddenly woke up and looked around. I was breathing heavily, and for a moment I didn't know where I was. Then I saw Brian on the other couch, and I must have woken him up because he opened his eyes. It quickly sank in that this wasn't just a bad dream and that we were still on the deck of the *Universal Explorer,* and that Alien-Bot was still out there somewhere looking for us.

Gor-Bot was standing in front of the large video monitor. When he noticed that we were awake, he came over and asked if everything was satisfactory. We said "yes" even though I wasn't really sure if it actually was.

"You must be hungry," he said. "I have a food replicator programmed with recipes from all over universe. Most of the ingredients are synthetic, so the texture and taste of the food isn't quite as satisfying as the real thing. Yet it is still filling and the nutrients are real, so they will provide you the nourishment you require. There are a few Earth recipes in there that Sven sent to me, although I don't care for some of his ethnic food like the raw sea herring or the caviar toothpaste. But I do enjoy the Swedish meatballs and pancakes."

"You eat too?" I asked. I shouldn't have been that surprised because I knew the Bots were part organic, but it still seemed strange because they looked mostly mechanical.

"Of course!" Gor-Bot said. "Our brains and hearts are still organic and need a source of energy, especially down in this cavern where one does not receive energy from sunlight.

Besides, our tongues are organic and have a very keen sense of taste, which is why our people still enjoy a good meal. At one time our chefs were among the finest in the universe, but that was before our galaxy started dying and our planet was no longer able to grow organic food. So we had to develop a synthetic nutrition source, but we wanted to make it as close to real food as possible because we still needed to feed our souls. So, I hope you will find the replicator satisfactory, but at the very least your energy will be boosted by eating. There is also a bathroom down below deck."

"You use a bathroom too?" I asked.

"Of course," Gor-Bot laughed.

I decided to use the bathroom before I ate and felt a lot better after doing so, especially when I splashed cold water on my face and in my hair. It felt like I had washed some of the space grime off, which was refreshing.

Brian used the bathroom after me, and then back up on deck Gor-Bot showed us how to use the food replicator. It looked like an oversized microwave oven with a video screen menu on the door. I found the Earth food section and ordered Swedish pancakes with butter, syrup, and whipped cream on top. The only drinks I recognized were orange juice,

apple juice, and Zonka Cola. Mommy and Daddy don't allow Parker and I to drink soda, so I had a Zonka Cola. Brian also had a Zonka Cola with his cheeseburger and French fries.

We sat at the old table in the middle of the deck and took hesitant bites of our food since we weren't sure if it was really going to taste like real Earth food. It was a little chewier than the real thing, but it wasn't bad. I was so hungry that after the first couple of bites I didn't even notice the chewiness. After we had finished eating, Gor-Bot cleared the table and said it was time to discuss our mission.

"I have detected the presence of intelligent life forms approaching in the tube," he said. "They are most likely the other cyborgs, and there are many of them. I am working under the assumption that their minds are not functioning independently and are under my son's control. They may not even be conscious like the two of you were when you arrived. Even if their minds are still their own, they may be disoriented and fearful, which would make their actions unpredictable and potentially dangerous. Fortunately their weapons systems may be inactive since my son probably anticipated that he would be the first to greet them, and it is not likely that they had someone like Sven on their home worlds to help activate them. Nevertheless, you must be ready to defend yourselves for any and all scenarios, including the possibility that they will attack."

Brian and I looked at each other worriedly, and then I looked back at Gor-Bot.

"What weapons should we use if they do attack?" I asked him.

"Use the power etherizer first," Gor-Bot said.

"The power etherizer?" I asked. "I never heard of that one."

"It is a blue laser that will temporarily put them into a deep sleep without harming them," Gor-Bot said. "If that does not work, you will simply have to allow your instincts to guide you."

"Like Duke Groundflyer and the Galactic

Laser Knights," Brian said. "*May the power of the positive possess your soul.*"

"I do not follow," Gor-Bot said.

"It's from a famous movie series called *Stellar Clashes*," I said. "I'm not that into it, but you might like it. It has all sorts of creatures from different galaxies and spaceships with laser shooters and stuff."

"It is the eternal battle of good versus evil that makes for box office magic," Brian said.

"It certainly sounds intriguing," Gor-Bot said. "I will be sure to look into it after our mission is complete. But we must now achieve total focus, so I want you to take everything I just told you and pack it into a box inside your head. Then I want you to close the lid of this box and move it off to the side where you can still see it, but where it will not get in your way. If the situation arises, you know that you can open this box and recall any of the information inside of it that you may need. Otherwise, leave it aside so that you can focus on your main task. If all goes according to plan, this task is relatively simple: you must administer a viral antidote code to each cyborg as they enter Alania's atmosphere."

"A viral antidote code?" Brian asked. "Intriguing."

"It is designed to infect any code that would give my son the ability to control their minds," Gor-Bot said. "It is essentially a computer virus that will tell them not to listen to him and to wait for further instructions from me. Once administered, the virus will put their minds on standby mode. The hope is that I will be able to capture my son and simply send them back to their home worlds, but I can also command them to assist us if necessary."

"How will we give them the virus?" I asked.

"I have upgraded your scanners to include an automated offline photonic transmitter that can upload the virus directly into their cyborg systems."

"An automated photonic transmitter?" Brian asked excitedly. "That is genius!"

"I like it too," Gor-Bot said. "It is something I designed when I was young, but I never had any use for it until now. The main reason for administering the virus this way is that photonic beams cannot be blocked with typical modern defense systems like laser walls or dampening fields. The only way to block a photonic beam would be to put a very dense physical object in front of it such as a thick wall made of steel or lead or some other impenetrable material. And since the transmitter is a small piece of offline hardware, my son will not be able to hack into it. Not even your own cyborg systems will be able to control it. The only way to turn it off is to physically remove it from your scanner and manually switch it to 'off'. As for its functionality, it will automatically detect and lock onto each target and fire the beam. All you have to do is navigate yourselves into position so that it can detect its targets, which is their cyborg eyes. The biggest challenge for you will be getting close enough to each cyborg. The transmitter needs to be within thirty feet in order to detect a target."

"Will we be able to tell how close we are to each target?" I asked.

"Yes," Gor-Bot said. "A distance meter will appear on your screen whenever you encounter another cyborg. When you get within thirty feet, the transmitter will work on its own. After the beam strikes its target, the upload will take less than a second and the cyborg should go right into standby mode. You will not need to take additional action.

"As for the cyborgs themselves, you will see a great variety of life forms that you have not seen before. Do not let this frighten you.

Also, do not be concerned if their faces are concealed by helmets similar to yours and you are unable to see their cyborg eyes. The transmitter will still detect their signals and the beam can travel through the helmet material. However, I do not think any will have armor like yours, which has been customized from the standard fire armor to enable space travel. I have actually never seen this sort of customization before."

"Sven modified it so we can travel in space," I said.

"Fascinating," Gor-Bot said. "Sven has a talent for applying our technology in new ways. We do not have armor that allows us to travel through space outside of a space vessel. I suppose it never even occurred to us since we have always used ships to travel."

"But Alien-Bot wasn't in a space vessel when he appeared in the wormhole above our school," Brian said.

"It is likely that he was inside a basic transport bubble and that his vessel was parked nearby," Gor-Bot said. "While it is possible that he has developed new technology that I am not yet aware of, whenever I've observed him traveling recently he has been using his regular vessel. That is why I suspect that the arriving cyborgs will each be inside one of these transport bubbles when they are passing through the tube. The bubbles are normally used in emergencies when someone accidentally winds up outside of a vessel while in deep space. They are pressurized and contain recyclable oxygen, and they can protect the passenger from the radiation and extreme cold of space. They can also be towed short distances with a basic retractor beam.

"In the past hour a new wormhole has opened near the ceiling of Alania's atmosphere, so I believe that the cyborgs will be arriving in a slightly different manner than the two of you did. They will initially arrive in the same section of space outside the tube that you did through individual wormholes. The reason my son did not have these wormholes open directly in our solar system is that there is simply not enough room for thousands of wormholes to open in this small area. Too many wormholes right next to each other could create a black hole. So he picked a large area of empty space in the main part of the universe where there is plenty of room, and he will tow the bubbles through the tube with retractor beams. You were also towed through the tube with retractor beams, but your armor allowed you to be towed at a much higher rate of speed than the relatively delicate bubbles can be towed with. This caused you to arrive much sooner than my son expected, and you had to travel through the airlock to get inside the atmosphere. The cyborgs in the bubbles will be passing through the new wormhole, thus allowing them to bypass the airlock. It would simply take too long to keep opening and closing the doors to allow thousands of cyborgs in. As soon as they pass through the threshold of the wormhole, the bubbles will burst simply because they were designed to be used in empty space and are unable to withstand the air pressure of our atmosphere. Even if the bubbles do not burst, the photonic beams can easily penetrate them."

"I have a question," Brian said. "Wouldn't it be easier to just keep a wormhole open all the time instead of using the airlock doors?"

"Because the atmosphere would slowly leak out," Gor-Bot said. "It is fine to have it open briefly, but the atmosphere needs to be tightly sealed inside the container."

"I have a question too," I said. "How will we be able to get close enough to the cyborgs for the photonic beam to fire? Will we just be hiding behind a rock somewhere and then run up to them when they land?"

"Oh, no," Gor-Bot said. "We cannot let them reach the surface. You must meet them at the wormhole near the ceiling."

"But how will we get up there?" Brian asked. "Will we be in a ship or a plane?"

"No," Gor-Bot said. "In addition to the photonic transmitter, I have also upgraded your abilities to include anti-gravitational propulsion."

"What is that?" I asked.

"It means we can fly," Brian said.

"We can fly?" I asked excitedly. "Yes! My dream has come true!"

"This is so," Gor-Bot said. "You will need to fly close enough to the target in order for the beam to fire."

"This is so awesome!" I said.

"Please remain calm," Gor-Bot said. "You must remain focused."

"So," Brian said, "we fly up to the wormhole, get within thirty feet of any cyborg that appears, the beam goes off, and the virus uploads. But then what will happen to the cyborgs we just beamed?"

"They will hold their position and remain in standby mode until I give them further instructions," Gor-Bot said. "The virus itself will still be performing tasks, such as building a complex firewall that will not allow my son to communicate with them or give them any commands. It will also give each of them the ability to create their own wormholes that will take them directly back to the last recorded location on their home worlds. It will even allow them to convert themselves back to their native organic state if they no longer wish to be cyborgs. Obviously it was wrong of my son to convert people into cyborgs without consent, so I wanted to make sure that they have the option of reversing this. I have also uploaded this same function to your own systems so that you too can convert yourselves back to your organic state if you wish."

"No!" Brian and I both yelled.

"I take it that both of you enjoy having cyborg abilities," Gor-Bot laughed. "You may certainly keep them if you wish. But everyone should have the option to choose what they do with their own bodies. My people were resistant to the technology at first, but when they finally tried it, they liked it—especially since it cured many of their ills and allowed them to live much longer lives."

"That sounds good to me!" I said. "And I like that I can use my abilities to help people.

That's why I wanted to become a super hero in the first place."

"You are a wise and noble human," Gor-Bot said. "Now, getting back to the mission, I have altered your cyborg signatures so that the arriving cyborgs will not recognize you as the fugitives my son is looking for. I do not know if he has commanded them to attack if they find you, but your signatures will actually be constantly changing into random identities. So, even if my son figures out one of these identities and commands the cyborgs to attack it, you will already have become someone else and they will leave you alone. I have also reprogrammed and relocated your signature codes so that even if my son is able to hack into your systems, he will not be able to easily find them. This should buy you enough time to complete your mission.

"While you are up near the wormhole, I will remain here and monitor your activities, as well as my son's. When I see the right opportunity, I will make my move to attempt capturing him. He will surely be distracted by the arriving cyborgs, as well as looking for the two of you, and since he presumably still believes that I am dead, I have the element of surprise on my side. I know his vulnerabilities better than anyone and I know what he is attempting to do, so I am certain that at some point an opportunity will present itself. I am also hoping that when he does eventually discover that I am still alive, it will cause a shock his system that will weaken his illness. So, when you are talking to each other up there, please do not mention my name or say anything to indicate that I am helping you. Hopefully I will be able to capture him quickly, and then we can send our cyborg friends back to their home worlds."

"Brilliant!" Brian said. "It seems like you have thought of everything!"

"I have tried to consider all possibilities and outcomes," Gor-Bot said. "That is something I always try to do whenever I have a decision to make."

Gor-Bot looked away for a moment. When he turned back to us, he looked sad.

"I know you are both nervous," he said. "I am nervous as well. It has been a long time since I have seen my son—my real son, Sci-Bot, not the evil being that has overtaken his mind. My greatest fear is that I will never see him again. Yet I still believe he is trapped in there and is trying to get out. I can feel it. I *must* save him."

Gor-Bot turned away again and looked at the monitors. I thought I heard him sniffle as if he was crying.

"Are you okay?" I asked.

Gor-Bot looked back at us.

"I am fine," he said. "The realization has entered my mind that I may have to take my son's life if one of Alien-Bot's actions threaten to destroy the universe. This is what I fear most. It is the worst nightmare of any parent to lose a child, but I cannot allow this beautiful universe or the wonderful people within it to die because of my son's illness."

I didn't know how to respond to this, and neither did Brian.

"I apologize for my emotions causing this distraction," Gor-Bot said. "We must remain focused on our specific tasks in order to accomplish our mission. If we get stuck on thinking about the bad possible outcomes, it will be more difficult to achieve the good ones we are working towards."

Gor-Bot paused and looked at us for a moment.

"It is time," he said. "Proceed to deploy your fire armor."

Brian and I looked at each other and then gave the command to deploy the armor. As scared as I should have been, seeing Gor-Bot looking at us with the proud sadness of a father sending his sons off to battle gave me a momentary feeling of brave confidence. I only wish my own dad was here to see us, and I wondered if Brian was thinking the same thing.

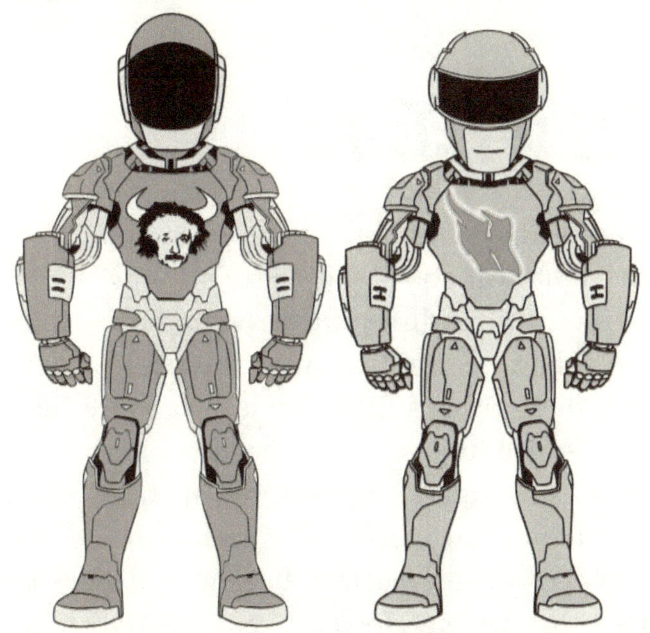

"You must go now," Gor-Bot said. "You are both very brave and noble young men. Hyperspeed, my friends. I will see you again very soon."

CHAPTER 11

Soaring up towards the new wormhole, I held my right arm above me with fist clenched and pointed in the direction we were headed, just like I had seen other super heroes do when they flew. Brian's flying style was more like a missile, leading with his head while holding both arms tightly against his sides. Looking down was scary, especially seeing the colorful splotches on the surface become smaller, so I tried to remain focused on the wormhole above us.

On the way up I didn't feel that afraid. All we had to do was get within thirty feet of any cyborg that emerged from the wormhole. I kept reminding myself of this over and over again and was confident that we could pull it off, especially since there were two of us. But when we pulled to a stop in front of the wormhole and waited, doubt began to creep in. I started thinking about my family back home and how I wished I was there instead of here, and that was enough to cause the small seed of doubt to quickly blossom into fear. I looked over at Brian and he seemed calm and focused on the wormhole, which helped me feel a little less afraid, but I needed more assurance.

"Are you scared?" I asked Brian.

"A little," he said. "It is perfectly natural to fear the unknown. But fear can be your friend too. Fear can be the thing that saves you from doing something stupid. If you weren't afraid, then you might be less careful and wind up doing something that will kill you."

I thought about that for a minute.

"I'm not sure that was very helpful," I said.

"You're thinking about it too much," Brian said. "When the action starts, you won't have time to think or be afraid. But when you're sitting around waiting for something to happen, your mind starts looking for something to stimulate it—especially minds like ours. It doesn't take long for it to find the fear and doubt just below the surface. It might be helpful if we just keep talking to each other, but we should talk about something else and keep the topic light so that our minds don't tighten up too much. At least that's what they do in those cop movies when they're sitting in the car waiting for the bad guys to come out. They usually make fun of each other or talk about funny stuff. Speaking of which, Mr. Cooldude said something funny about Mrs. Crabcake when I was talking to him. He said that one day a long time ago he was out surfing in California when something bumped into his surfboard and knocked him off. At first he was afraid it was a shark, but when he looked around he saw a strange creature swimming back out to sea. The creature's head was sticking out of the water, and it looked very much like a human head with hair just like Mrs. Crabcake's. Then he started asking about what she was like as a teacher and if I remembered her saying or doing anything unusual. It was really weird. It almost felt like I was being questioned by a cop."

"Did you know that Mr. Cooldude's file is classified?" I asked.

"No," he said. "How do you know that?"

"I thought it was weird that a total surfer dude from California would move to a cold weather place like West Plains, so I did a search for him in my cyborg system. It said that he went to Clairemont High School in San Diego, but the rest of the file was classified."

"Interesting," Brian said. "I wonder if he works for the C.I.A. or something and is investigating Mrs. Crabcake."

Suddenly out of the corner of my eye I saw a small green light appear in the opening of the wormhole.

"Look," I said calmly while pointing towards the wormhole.

"That must be our first arrival," Brian said.

I used my cyborg super vision to zoom in on the light and found myself looking at the strangest living being I had ever seen. It was a glowing neon green blob with a single cyborg eye surrounded by a cyborg facemask. It didn't even have arms or legs or a mouth or anything besides the eye. It was inside of a transport bubble at first, but the bubble popped as soon as it cleared the opening of the wormhole.

"What the heck?" I said.

"Just slowly move closer," Brian said, "and don't get distracted by its appearance. We're probably going to see all sorts of crazy looking aliens emerging from that wormhole. This one looks like an easy target, so why don't you take it. I've got your back if it tries something, and

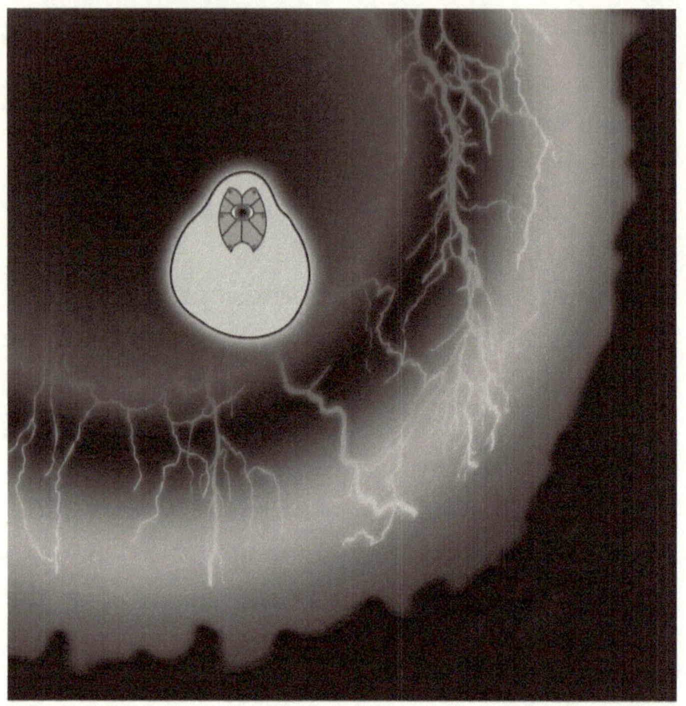

I'll also be watching the wormhole if another one shows up."

I took a deep breath and slowly flew towards a spot where I thought I could get out in front of the blob and block its path. Flying was actually pretty easy and kind of like walking because I didn't really even have to think about it—I just knew where I had to go and started moving in that direction. On the bottom of my cyborg screen it said "DISTANCE TO CYBORG: 500 FEET", and the number decreased as I got closer. But the blob was moving much faster than it seemed to be from far away, and I soon realized that I would have to speed up to get out in front of it.

"Faster!" Brian said, which made me nervous. "Don't let him get past you!"

I increased my speed, but I didn't really know how fast I could or should go. I was still 200 feet away when the blob passed through the original spot where I thought I would intercept it. I didn't know what to do, but finally Brian said, "I'll get him!" and shot out in front of the blob at hyperspeed. He stopped at a spot that looked to be about 100 feet in front of it and waited in its path.

Then I noticed that the blob's cyborg eye was glowing brighter and quickly realized that it was scanning Brian. I got worried that it might attack him, so without even thinking about it I shot out at hyperspeed towards the blob and was ready to blast him with the power etherizer. But Brian must have noticed the blob's eye as well because he suddenly flew right towards it at high speed. Just when it looked like they were about to have a head-on collision, a bright flash suddenly lit the sky and a beam shot out from Brian's scanner right into the blob's cyborg eye. The blob came to a full stop, and for a moment it looked like the beam was holding it in place. But then the beam suddenly disappeared and the blob remained

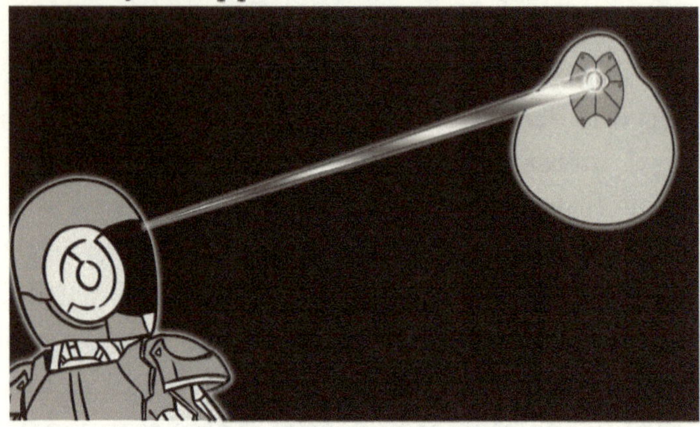

motionless. It didn't seem to be hurt and its eye was still glowing. Like Gor-Bot had said would happen, it appeared to be looking at Brian as if awaiting further instructions.

"Got him!" Brian said. "Or her."

"What is it going to do now?" I asked.

"I guess just wait there until Gor-Bot sends instructions," Brian said. "Whoa, lookout!"

I turned towards the wormhole and saw a giant sasquatch cyborg with huge claws on its hands and feet heading directly towards me at a much faster speed than the blob had been moving. This one was already out of the wormhole and wasn't inside a transport bubble. His arms were positioned above his head as if ready to attack and he was moving so fast that my first instinct was to get out of the way, but I couldn't move. It almost felt like something inside my mind was holding me in place. The "DISTANCE TO CYBORG" number was quickly decreasing, and when it changed from three digits to two I closed my eyes and braced for impact. A couple of seconds went by before I heard a brief humming noise like something was powering up. Then there was a buzz and a bright flash that I could see even with my eyes closed. I opened my eyes and saw the sasquatch being held in place by the

photonic beam shooting from my scanner. The beam then suddenly disappeared and a message popped up on my cyborg screen: "UPLOAD SUCCESSFUL". The "DISTANCE TO CYBORG" was stopped at ten feet, and the sasquatch now looked calm with his arms down at its sides.

"Nice shootin', Tex!" Brian said. "That guy was moving fast!"

"Woo-hoo!" I cheered, suddenly feeling energized and confident. Even though it was a close call, my fear was gone and I was ready for another cyborg to appear. Or so I thought…

The next one to emerge from the wormhole looked human in form and had the same kind of armor as us except it was shiny pink with a gold "S" logo on top of a black star. But this one was not floating in a nice straight line like the other cyborgs and was instead wobbling from side to side as if out of control and frantically waving its arms above its head.

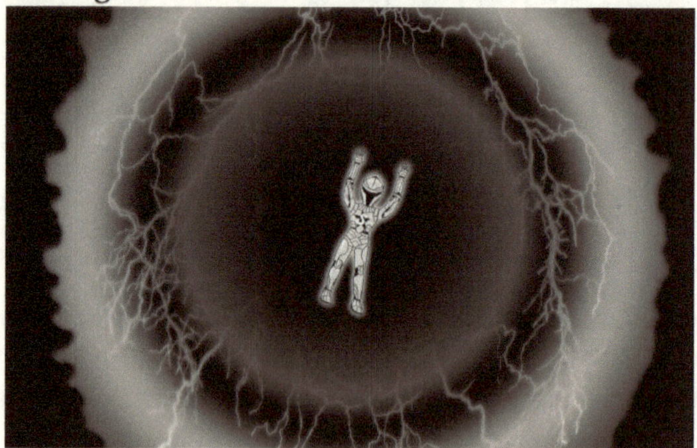

"Help!" a girl's voice suddenly screamed in our intercoms. Before we could even respond, she screamed again as she hurtled towards us. She was moving so wildly and so fast that it was hard to tell where we had to position ourselves in order to intercept her.

"Don't just sit there on your lazy butts!" she yelled. "Help me!"

"Morgan, move over to your right," Brian said calmly. "I'll move to the left. This way she'll get within range of one of us."

"Roger," I said confidently. But before I even had a chance to move, she suddenly dropped into a freefall towards the surface as if she had fallen off the side of a cliff.

She screamed again and then yelled, "Will one of you fools help me before I splat all over the ground? That would *not* be a good look for me!"

"On my way!" Brian said and suddenly shot down towards her like a missile. On his way down he said, "Morgan, you take over and beam the cyborgs. I'll be back as soon as I can."

"Okay," I said shakily. For a moment I felt very scared at being left alone as I watched Brian race towards the girl, but that fear vanished when I noticed that several more cyborgs had emerged from the wormhole.

The closest one looked like a reptile with a human-shaped body. Fortunately it was moving slowly and steadily, so I was able to fly into range and beam it without any difficulty.

The next one was a small blue creature that almost looked like a fish with arms, and I was able to easily beam that one as well.

Then there was one that looked very much like a human except that it kept changing colors like a chameleon and suddenly became invisible just before I got into range. I stopped and looked around for a moment, and when it didn't reappear I resumed flying in the direction where I thought it was headed. I used the "DISTANCE TO CYBORG" meter to figure out where it was by heading in the direction that made the number decrease. I was worried that the photonic transmitter wouldn't work if the cyborg was still invisible, but fortunately it did because the beam fired as soon as the meter hit thirty feet.

Dozens of cyborgs of all shapes, sizes, and colors came through one after the other, and none of them gave me much difficulty. After a while I started feeling confident that I could handle this by myself, but then the stream of cyborgs stopped and I didn't know what to do next.

After waiting several minutes, fear started to creep back in. Having no one to talk to and seeing all the cyborgs floating in standby mode who could at any moment be instructed by

Alien-Bot to attack me was a really scary thought. Eventually I called out to Brian on the intercom, but he did not answer.

Originally I was expecting hundreds or thousands or even millions of cyborgs to come through the wormhole because of what Gor-Bot had said about there being "many" of them in the tube, but I began to wonder if this was all of them. If it was, I didn't know if I should stay there and wait or head down to the surface where Brian and the girl with the armor had disappeared from view. It was really hard to stay focused because it felt like I should be doing something. The longer I looked down at the ground, the more tempted I was to go down there.

But the decision was made for me when I heard a loud roar come from the direction of the wormhole. I turned my head to see a ginormous green dragon cyborg flapping its wings and shooting flames from its mouth and nostrils. I had never seen a creature this large in my life. It was probably even bigger than Sven's Viking ship. It was so large that even from 200 feet away I felt like I was right next to it and was afraid to get any closer.

Fortunately it was moving slowly, and after watching it for a minute I began to realize that it meant no harm. Its wings made a loud "whooshing" noise as they smoothly flapped up and down, and the puffs of fire now coming from its nostrils seemed only to be part of its normal breathing process. I also sensed that it didn't know what was happening and that it was scared, which is probably why it roared and shot fire from its mouth when it first emerged from the wormhole.

I knew I had to be careful not to spook it, so I started flying alongside it from about 200 feet away at a speed fast enough to get out ahead of it. Fortunately it didn't react as I passed by, so I sped up a little more and turned slightly inward so that I would eventually get to a spot directly in its path. I stopped 200 feet in front of it and waited as it slowly approached, but when it was fifty feet away it suddenly pulled to a stop.

"It's okay, dragon," I said out loud, hoping that maybe it had an intercom and could understand me. "I don't want to hurt you, I just want to help you get back home. But first I need to fix your cyborg system with a laser beam. I promise it won't hurt."

The dragon responded with a noise similar to the trumpet-like sound that elephants make, and I sensed that it was telling me that it understood. Just to be sure, I asked my cyborg system for a translation, but the word "SEARCHING" appeared on my screen and kept blinking over and over again. After a few seconds I just canceled the search. I didn't need a computer to confirm what I already knew.

"Okay, dragon," I said out loud. "Do you have a name? Maybe I'll just call you 'Fire-Bot'. I have to move a little closer, Fire-Bot, and then a laser beam is going to shoot from my forehead into your cyborg eye. It will only take a second, and I promise it won't hurt. Then me and my friends are going to help you get back home."

The dragon responded with the elephant noise again, which convinced me even more that it understood me. As slowly as I could, I started flying towards it and watched the distance meter tick down to thirty feet. Suddenly the photonic beam flashed and startled the dragon, and it let out a huge roar that startled me back. Flames shot out of its mouth and came right at me, but my armor protected me and the wall of fire harmlessly passed right by. The upload only took a second, but it felt more like an hour.

The "UPLOAD SUCCESSFUL" message appeared on my screen, and suddenly

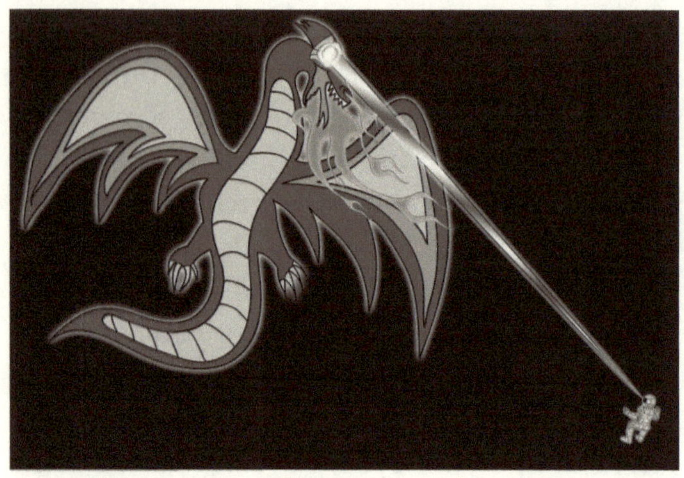

everything was calm again. The dragon was floating in standby mode like the other cyborgs. I looked at it for a few seconds and it began to sink in that I was face to face with a real fire-breathing dragon. Then I remembered my transformation scanner and scanned the dragon so that I could transform into it later if I had to.

There was no more activity in the wormhole, so to pass the time I started scanning the rest of the floating cyborgs. Every few seconds I turned and looked back at the wormhole, but all was quiet. After I had scanned them all, I again started feeling anxious about not knowing what to do, so I used my cyborg vision to zoom in on the surface hoping to see a sign that Brian was coming back. I also zoomed in on the city under the blue dome, including Alien-Bot's house. All appeared to be quiet, and I was about to look away when an extremely bright light flashed from Alien-Bot's property and momentarily blinded me.

"What the heck?" I said out loud. "Brian, can you hear me? BullBorg, come in BullBorg! Please answer me! There was a bright flash at Alien-Bot's house! Come in Brian! Can you hear me?"

"I can hear you loud and clear, Mr. Earth Super Hero," said a voice in my intercom that I immediately recognized as Alien-Bot's.

CHAPTER 12

"Help!" I yelled into my intercom. "Alien-Bot is coming after me! Help!"

"On my way, Hot Pants!"

I looked down and saw the girl with the pink armor flying up towards me at

hyperspeed, but Brian wasn't with her. When she arrived at my position, she looked around and then back at me.

"Where's this Alien-Bot dude you're shouting about, Hot Pants?" she asked. "And why are you just sitting up here on your butt doing nothing?"

"Where's Brian?" I asked worriedly. "And who are you?"

"Stella Bella SuperStar is here to save your butt, Hot Pants!" she said. "BBP is busy doing some computer stuff. He installed some upgrades for me and said I should fly up here to help you beam some cyborgs. I can't believe I can fly now! Maybe I should change my name to 'Stella Bella SuperFly'!"

"Who's 'BBP'?" I asked.

"Sorry," she laughed. "That's just a nickname me and my friends gave BullBorg. It stands for 'Beefcake Booty Pants'. We call you 'Hot Pants'."

"You know who we are?" I asked.

"Of course!" she laughed. "Everybody knows who you guys are!"

"Do you live in West Plains?" I asked.

"West Plains? Heck no! I live in New York City. Harlem, baby! Sugar Hill in the house!"

I had a million more questions to ask her,

especially since we used to live in Harlem when I was little before we moved to West Plains, but a cyborg had appeared in the wormhole, and then another.

"Looks like we have company," I said. "Do you know what to do?"

"Sure do, Hot Pants!" she said. "Just get within thirty feet. No problemo! Stella Bella SuperStar has got this!"

A steady stream of cyborgs now began pouring out of the wormhole. By the time we got to the ones at the front of the pack, there were at least twenty more behind them and new ones were appearing continuously without any signs of letting up.

I was expecting Stella to be hesitant at first like I had been, but she flew right up to and beamed a cyborg that had a humanlike body except for the four arms and metallic silver skin. Her beam then went off again right away because there was already another cyborg within thirty feet of her. She then zoomed over to another one and the beam went off again. I was so stunned at seeing how quickly she worked that I didn't realize I was just watching and not beaming any cyborgs myself.

"Let's go, Hot Pants!" she said. "We have work to do!"

It was amazing how quickly Stella flew from target to target and how totally focused she was. She was able to go from a full stop to hyperspeed and from hyperspeed to a full stop. As soon as each upload was complete, she would immediately zoom over to the next one. I knew I couldn't fly fast like her and started feeling frustrated.

"I can't fly that fast!" I said.

"I didn't know I could either!" she said. "Just go to the middle of the pack and get as many as you can and I'll catch up to you. Don't worry, Hot Pants, we got this!"

I flew over towards the middle of the river of cyborgs that was spilling out of the wormhole and beamed a cyborg that looked like a reptilian cat with six legs and a pair of wings. Next I beamed one that looked like a giant millipede, and then another that was just a black cube with a cyborg mask. After each upload I stopped and tried to figure out which one to go to next, but it was difficult because there were so many of them and it was hard to tell which one was the closest. When I did finally pick one I would start flying towards it, but then I would get distracted by seeing another one that looked closer and would change course.

In the distance I saw Stella working quickly, which made me feel like I should be working faster. But every time I sped up, I missed the spot I was aiming for and would then have to stop and go back. This is how I often felt during tests when the other kids finished before me. I felt like I had to work faster, but that only caused me to panic and lose focus and I would start having difficulty even with stuff that I knew.

While I was struggling to get from one cyborg to the next, somewhere buried in the noise and confusion in my mind I heard the distant echo of voices calling my name. I stopped flying so I could focus on the voices, which at first sounded very far away. Now they started sounding clearer and seemed to be getting closer, and soon I could tell it was Mommy and Daddy. They were saying what they always said when I tried to do something too fast: *Morgan, don't rush... slow down... focus on one thing at a time...* They would often tell me to stop for a moment and take a deep breath, which always annoyed me at first but it usually did work. I would close my eyes and breathe in as deep as I could, then exhale as slowly as possible. When I opened my eyes again it felt as if the room had become calmer, which enabled me to focus on what was directly in front of me and to stop being distracted by how much I still had left to do.

So now, here in the deepest part of outer space that any human had ever traveled, I closed my eyes and took a deep breath. I slowly exhaled, and as I did so my body began to relax. When I opened my eyes again a few seconds later, they immediately focused on a giant cyborg parrot 45 feet away that had feathers of every color imaginable. There were many more cyborgs in my field of vision, but they were blurry in the background and the parrot was the only one I was clearly seeing. Without even thinking about it, my body just calmly started drifting towards the parrot and it felt like I was moving without any effort at all. My instincts had totally taken over, and by focusing totally on the parrot I was able to keep my conscious mind from distracting my body from what it was doing. I was so focused on the parrot that I didn't even notice that the distance meter had hit thirty feet, so I was a bit startled when the beam fired.

I then turned to my left and my eyes immediately landed on a bright green cyborg that looked like a classic movie alien with the big head, giant eyes, and skinny body. Once again I was able to focus on one cyborg while the rest were just a blur in the background. Calmly I drifted towards it until the beam went off and the "UPLOAD SUCCESSFUL" message appeared on my screen.

I kept doing this over and over again, focusing on the first cyborg my eyes landed on and drifting towards it until the beam went off. It seemed like I wasn't putting any thought or effort into it at all. I just allowed my eyes to show my body where to go. Everything seemed to be moving in slow motion.

"Now you're moving, Hot Pants!" Stella said, breaking my concentration and causing me to stop. "Now *I* can't keep up with *you*!"

"What?" I asked, looking around and seeing that Stella had beamed the last cyborg in her section, but she was still about a hundred feet away. Without even realizing it, I had already worked my way to the wormhole entrance. I waited for Stella to zoom over, and she suggested that we just start beaming the cyborgs as they emerge from the wormhole and that she would work the left half while I worked the right. The cyborgs were still flowing out of the wormhole, but now it was more like a calm stream than a raging river.

While Stella zoomed over to her side and

beamed her first cyborg, I closed my eyes and took another slow deep breath. When I opened them again my eyes landed on a cyborg tree with glowing purple and blue leaves and a facemask high up on its neon green trunk. After beaming the tree, I just let my eyes land on the next cyborg and once again I was in the zone I had been in earlier. I don't know how many more cyborgs I beamed, but the next thing I knew I found myself floating in the middle next to Stella with no more cyborgs left to beam.

"Nice work, Hot Pants!" she said and gave me a high five. Our armor-covered hands clanked as they made contact, but at that same moment the wormhole started thundering loudly and the blue lightning lining the interior walls started sparking erratically.

"Get back!" I yelled. We both zoomed away from the wormhole at hyperspeed just before it collapsed and disappeared. Suddenly there was silence except for the faint electric hum of the atmosphere shield above us.

"Woohoo, we did it!" Stella shouted, triumphantly raising her arms above her head.

"There must be a thousand of them," I said, looking around at the cyborgs floating in limbo all around us. "But at least it's not a million."

"Now what?" Stella asked. "Am I supposed to just float here and look pretty?"

I laughed, and Stella laughed too. I hadn't even seen what she looked like under her armor, but I sensed that she was pretty.

"I used to live in Harlem when I was little," I said.

"For real?" Stella said. "You're a city kid? I thought you were a country boy."

"Well, West Plains isn't really the country," I said. "I've never even seen a cow in West Plains. It's actually not even that far from the city. That's why it seems strange that you know about us but we don't know about you. Why haven't we heard of you before?"

Stella didn't answer at first, but eventually she said, "That's kind of a long story." She sounded sad and I could tell that she didn't want to talk about it, so I decided to change the subject. I was about to ask about her armor when there was a bright flash down on the surface around where Brian had flown to catch Stella. The flash was similar to the one I had seen near Alien-Bot's house.

"What the—" Stella started, but she was cut off by an explosion behind us. We turned and saw that a new wormhole had opened that was only big enough for one or two people. I hoped that maybe Brian or Gor-Bot might emerge, but this hope quickly turned to fear when I saw the familiar red eyes staring back at us from the darkness inside the wormhole.

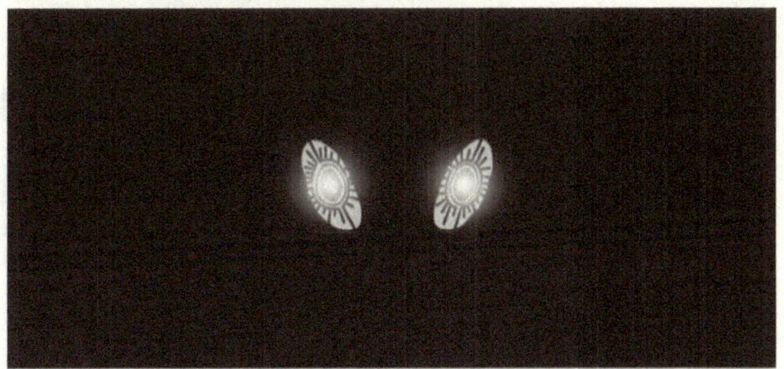

"Who is that?" Stella asked quietly. I could tell she was scared, and I was scared too, especially since I knew who it was. But I was also starting to feel mad. I was tired of this. This bully had no right to hurt so many people just because he thought his world was more important than all the other worlds in the universe.

"I see you hiding in there," I said. "I'm not afraid of you."

"Me neither," Stella said.

The figure floated slowly out of the darkness, but I suddenly wasn't so sure if it was the real Alien-Bot or some kind of clone. His body was not the usual steel gray but was now shiny gold, and my cyborg system identified him as "UNKNOWN". He was also surrounded by a glowing red laser force field similar to the atmosphere shield. But after zooming in close on his face, I knew I was looking at none other than Alien-Bot himself.

"Now I have you," he said calmly. "And also your new little friend here. But what a waste. I should have known better than to use my meteors on ignorant Earth children to join my new paradise. I do not understand why you meddling kids are so determined to resist, but no matter. I and I alone am in charge of this great society, and anyone who questions me will face the same doom that you now face. As soon as I clear the two of you out of the way, I can repair my new cyborg subjects that you temporarily subdued with that silly little virus you concocted, and then I can finally execute my plans without further interruption. Your journey has reached its end, HyperChild, just as it did for your little Earth playmate BullBoy. Are you sure you do not wish to reconsider pledging your allegiance to me? Or are you going to challenge me to the end as he did?"

"No!" I cried. My mind started racing with the thought that Brian might be gone, but it suddenly stopped cold when I thought I heard his voice inside my mind. The voice was faint, but I realized that he might be speaking to me telepathically like he did back in Alien-Bot's jail cell. I tried to block out all the other noise and static in my mind and focus only on his voice, but it was difficult. I was determined, though, and this determination was the fuel I needed to keep fighting through the clutter and push it aside. It almost felt like I was fighting my way through a thick jungle, but eventually I reached a clearing where I was able to focus on his voice and hear him loud and clear.

"Don't worry, I'm okay," Brian's voice said. "Alien-Bot did try to attack me, but it was a trap we set to distract him from finding Gor-Bot's cavern. I tricked him the same way Gor-Bot tricked him with a fake self-destruct bomb, so he thinks I'm dead. Just play along and act like you're mad at him for killing me and try to keep him distracted as long as you can. Gor-Bot is almost finished with a hack that will disable his armor and make him virtually powerless. Then you'll be able to stop him with the power etherizer."

Alien-Bot's voice then brought me out of my deep focus.

"I take your silence as a final rejection of my generous offer," he said. "It is unfortunate that you Earth aliens will not be part of my great new civilization, especially since your minds have such enormous potential. But this is not a democracy. There will be no place in this society for young upstarts who do not obey their supreme leader."

Even though Alien-Bot was in the middle of threatening us, I couldn't help noticing how cool his golden armor looked and decided to scan him so that I could transform into him later. But when I tried to do the scan, an error message appeared saying that it was unsuccessful.

Alien-Bot let out a wicked robotic laugh.

"Earthen fool!" he said. "Do you really think I would appear before you knowing that you have scanner transformation abilities? Considering that you and your hooligan friend BullBoy were clever enough to create that silly little virus, I would not have expected you to attempt something so utterly unintelligent. But now I see that you are nothing more than an ignorant oversized infant. Sad!"

"Nobody speaks to my friends that way, Alien-Butt!" Stella said. "Especially someone with such a butt-ugly gold plating job! That's not even real gold! I can tell because I know all about gold and jewelry, and it looks like you just sprayed yourself with a can of cheap spray paint you got from the corner hardware store. My my, that *is* a fashion faux pas if I ever did see one. Did you have your eyes closed when you sprayed yourself? Or did you learn plating by watching how-to videos on ViewCube? And another thing—your butt stinks!"

"Silence!" Alien-Bot commanded.

"Don't you tell me to silence, Ugly-Bot!" Stella said.

This time Alien-Bot didn't respond, and I suddenly had a strong feeling that he was about to attack Stella.

"Lookout, Stella!" I shouted just before

Alien-Bot fired a laser beam at her. Fortunately she reacted quickly to my warning and was able to get out of the way.

Now I was really angry, but my mind was crystal clear because I knew exactly what I had to do. I quickly searched my newly updated catalogue of transformation scans and found the one I wanted, then gave the command to transform. Because the dragon's body was so big, the transformation took a little longer than it did when I transformed into Ralston. But it was totally worth it. Alien-Bot now looked to me like a puny little bug.

"Whoa, Dragon Pants!" Stella laughed. "Now you've got that spray painted squid-butt right where you want him, so go get him!"

"How can this be?" Alien-Bot wondered aloud as if he had forgotten that we could hear him. "The cyborgs are unscannable. How did these foolish children get around my firewalls? No one can get around my firewalls except... no, it cannot be..."

The dragon's cyborg system interface was the same as mine, but the blaster options were different. There were only three choices:

FIRE BREATH
LASER EYE POWER BLASTER
HEALER RAY

I didn't think the fire breath would be strong enough because it didn't damage my own fire armor when the real dragon shot flames at me, and the healer ray was probably only meant for physical injuries and not mental illness. So, there was really no choice.

After selecting LASER EYE POWER BLASTER, the target crosshairs appeared on my screen and I focused on Alien-Bot. When the target locked onto his chest, the red "FIRE" button appeared in the lower right corner of the screen.

Even though I was now locked and loaded, I didn't shoot. Something didn't feel right. Alien-Bot wasn't even looking at me, nor was he looking at Stella. His head was hung as if he was looking at something down on the surface, but I couldn't tell what it could be. I sensed that he was confused.

"What are you waiting for?" Stella yelled. "Get him!"

Stella's command snapped Alien-Bot out of his trance. As he slowly turned his head towards her, a message appeared on my screen:

WEAPON SYSTEM DETECTED

This time I didn't hesitate. My blaster fired

a single shot that struck Alien-Bot right in the middle of his chest and sent him reeling backwards. Sparks and flames spewed from the charred crater that was now in the middle of his chest. Torn wires and twisted metal shards were visible between the sparks. A red streak that looked like blood had stained a patch of smooth gold plating next to the crater.

What I didn't know was that just before I fired, Gor-Bot had finished disabling Alien-Bot's laser shield and all of his defense systems. This meant that he had been totally defenseless when the dragon's powerful laser blast struck him. I was unaware of how badly he was actually hurt and was expecting him to fire back at me, so I moved into position and locked in on him again. I was about to fire when a voice in my intercom loudly commanded, "Stop! Hold your fire!"

It took me a moment to realize that the voice was Gor-Bot's. I looked around but didn't see him or Brian. I then turned back to Alien-Bot and saw that he was now motionless and slowly drifting away. The frayed wires dangling from the crater in his chest were no longer sparking, and his eyes were now dim and lifeless. Suddenly I was overcome with a terrible fear that I had killed him.

"Father?" a voice whispered in the intercom. It was barely audible, but I knew right away that it was Alien-Bot. I was relieved that he was still alive, but he sounded very weak.

"How can this be?" he continued. "Father, you were killed by... Alien-Bot."

"It is I, Sci-Bot," Gor-Bot said. "I was not killed. I am alive and well and wish to help you. But Alien-Bot must surrender at once."

"Yes, Father," he said. "Sci-Bot has returned. Alien-Bot surrenders."

CHAPTER 13

A new wormhole opened near Alien-Bot, and moments later Gor-Bot and Brian emerged from it. Gor-Bot quickly flew over to his son while Brian coasted over to where Stella and I were waiting. I had already transformed back to my human form with armor deployed and watched as Gor-Bot tended to his son. I felt sick that I had seriously injured him.

"I wasn't trying to kill him!" I said to Brian. I was starting to cry. "I was just defending Stella! He was about to attack her!"

"I know," Brian said calmly. He floated over and put his hand on my shoulder. "We saw the whole thing. Gor-Bot has already run a remote diagnostic scan on Alien-Bot that showed no critical injuries to his organic parts, and that the damaged mechanical parts are easily replaceable."

"But I saw blood!" I cried.

"It was just a small flesh wound to some non-critical organic tissue," Brian said. "Gor-Bot seems pretty sure that he'll be fine."

"Is Gor-Bot mad at me?" I asked.

"No, of course not," Brian said, sounding surprised. "Why would he be mad at you?"

"Because I almost killed his son!" I said. I couldn't hold it in any longer and started crying uncontrollably.

"But you did it to save me!" Stella said. "He might have killed me if you didn't shoot!" She then floated closer and hugged me, which wasn't an easy thing to do in our bulky armor. Brian also put an arm around me and I put my arms around them so that we were huddled together like a small interstellar football team.

"You saved the universe without killing anyone," Brian said. "Gor-Bot said you made the perfect shot to stop Alien-Bot without permanently damaging him. You saved everyone back home, including your mother and father and brother, as well as my mother and Stella's family and all the other people in the universe and their families. You're like the greatest super hero of all time!"

"You guys helped too," I said.

"It was perfect teamwork," Brian said. "That's what happens when people work together instead of against one another."

I watched as Gor-Bot used his tentacles to strap his son onto his back. Even though Brian said the injuries were not life-threatening, I was still worried and sent Gor-Bot a text message through my cyborg system telling him that I was sorry and asking if Sci-Bot was badly hurt. Instead of responding by text, Gor-Bot spoke through the intercom.

"There is no need to apologize," he said. "I witnessed the entire event and fully understand that you were not only defending yourselves, you were defending the entire universe. You accomplished your mission with bravery, valor, and compassion. I am very proud of all of you, and you should be proud of yourselves. As for my son, I have already healed his flesh wound and am confident he will fully recover after I complete repairs to his cyborg systems. I will now bring him to the lab at his house and work on him there. In the meantime, the three of you must help these cyborgs get back to their home worlds. After this task is completed, please proceed to my son's house. I will deactivate the defense systems on the property before your arrival."

The three of us watched Gor-Bot, with Sci-Bot secured on his back as if on a stretcher, slowly descend towards the blue dome. Even though Gor-Bot had assured me that Sci-Bot would recover, I still felt upset that I had almost killed him.

"Are you alright, Morgan?" Brian asked.

"I think so," I said. "I just can't stop thinking about how I almost killed Sci-Bot."

"But you didn't kill him," Stella said. "You heard the old guy. He's gonna be fine. And you saved everyone in the universe. You're a true super hero, Hot Pants!"

"She's right, Morgan," Brian said. "But now you need to find your focus again because we still have to get these cyborgs home."

"What do we need to do?" I asked.

"Gor-Bot gave me some code to upload to their cyborg systems," Brian said. "The code will open wormholes for each of them that will lead them directly back to the exact spot on their home planets where they were taken from. The wormholes will open right here, so they won't even have to go back through the tube again. And we won't need to use the photonic transmitters to upload the code since Alien-Bot will no longer be trying to stop us. I can transmit it to all of them at once over an open channel, so it will be quick. But I need you guys to keep an eye out just in case something goes wrong."

"Didn't Gor-Bot say it was dangerous to open too many wormholes in the same place?" I asked.

"He said it would be okay for the short-term," Brian said. "Alien-Bot was being extra cautious because this solar system is very delicate and he didn't want to cause any long-term damage with lots of wormholes, but that no longer matters. Are you guys ready?"

Stella and I said yes, and the three of us turned our attention towards the large group of silently hovering cyborgs. For those whose faces we could see, it was pretty obvious that they did not know what was happening. It was creepy to think that they had been brainwashed by a tyrant who was willing to destroy the universe in order to build some sort of fake paradise for them. It was also scary to think what would have happened if our minds had been unable to resist being brainwashed. We might have wound up among them and would have been powerless to fight back and stop him.

"Let's send them home," I said.

"Roger," Brian said. "I'm transmitting the code now."

Moments later a small wormhole opened and the little green blob cyborg emerged from the pack and slowly floated towards it. Then another wormhole opened, and another, and soon the sky was filled with them. Individual cyborgs began to emerge from the pack and float towards whichever wormhole was theirs. After disappearing inside, the wormhole would silently collapse into nothing as if it had never even been there. The whole process seemed very orderly and reminded me of people politely exiting a crowded movie theater.

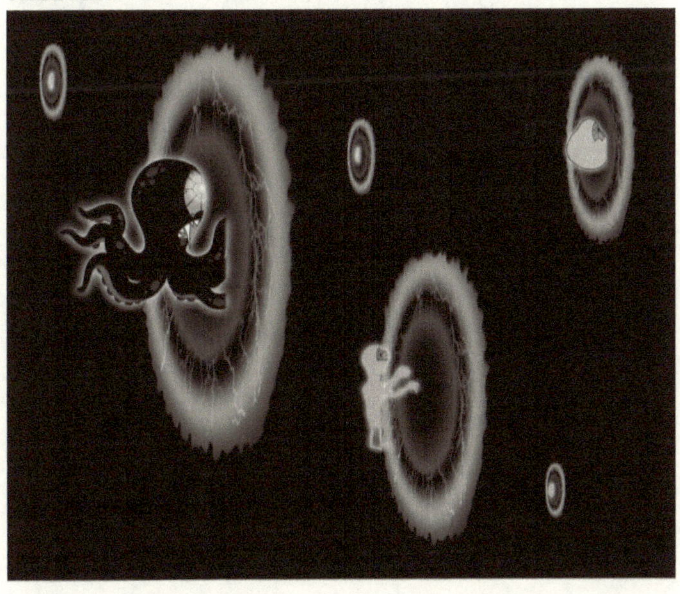

All but one of the cyborgs exited without turning towards us. A large wormhole had opened for the dragon, but he didn't float directly towards it as the others had done. Instead he stopped, looked right at me, and made the trumpet noise. I knew he was asking if we needed his help.

"You can go home now, Fire-Bot," I said. "And thanks for your help! I'll never forget you!"

The dragon trumpeted again, then turned towards his wormhole and disappeared inside.

After the last wormhole had closed, the sky was empty and silent. For the first time since arriving at Alania I felt a sense of peace when looking down at its surface.

"Did you understand the dragon?" Stella asked.

"I think he said 'thank you, friendly alien creatures'," I explained. I didn't know if those were his exact words, but I knew that's what he meant.

"Do you think the cyborgs will remember any of this?" Stella asked.

"I don't know," Brian said. "I'm guessing that it will seem like a really strange dream."

"At least now they'll be able to decide for themselves if they want to stay cyborgs," I said.

"I'll never give up my powers!" Stella said. "I'm gonna use them to become a movie star and a fashion designer and I'm gonna be rich and buy a huge penthouse overlooking Central Park and also a big mansion in the country, and I'll have huge closets in both places with all different super hero outfits and shoes and I'll wear a different outfit whenever I make an appearance in public and—"

"Let's go see how Gor-Bot is doing with his son," Brian interrupted.

"Yes," I said. "And then I want to go home too."

CHAPTER 14

Under the dome of the empty city we flew over the vacant buildings and houses until the deep blue grass of Sci-Bot's great lawn came into view. The red laser wall surrounding the property was now gone, which made the big white mansion on the hill appear much more inviting than the last time we were there.

After landing on the grass near the front entrance and retracting our armor, Brian and I finally got our first look at Stella Bella SuperStar. All along I had a feeling that she was pretty, but that didn't prepare me for how pretty she actually turned out to be. She was totally the most beautiful girl I had ever seen, and judging by the way Brian was looking at her, he probably thought so too. She was African-American, had long wavy hair that was styled perfectly even though she had just been wearing a helmet, and she was wearing makeup. She looked like a movie star or a famous singer, and although she seemed to be about the same size as other fifth grade girls, the hair and makeup made her look a lot older. And while Brian and I were wearing our regular school clothes, she was wearing a pink super hero costume with a black cape and the same "S" logo that was on her fire armor. Her cyborg eye was glowing bright pink through the eyehole of a diamond-studded masquerade mask. Her cyborg facemask and arm were plated with shiny gold, which was really cool compared to the dull industrial gray steel cyborg parts that Brian and I had.

"How come you guys aren't wearing your super hero outfits?" she asked.

"We came here straight from school," I said. "Umm… wouldn't you have been in school too if you were abducted at the same time as us?"

"I was at school!" she said. "Don't tell anyone this, but I'm a straight A student. I wouldn't miss school even if I was deathly ill."

"Then why are you wearing your super hero costume?" Brian asked.

"This *outfit* is what I wore to school!" she said. "Are you guys saying that you don't wear your super hero outfits to school? Don't you guys know about branding and publicity?"

"My parents don't let me wear my costume to school," I said.

"My mother doesn't let me either," Brian said.

"For real?" Stella said. "Maybe you guys should hire an agent who could negotiate that for you. An agent could also get you some serious paying gigs. I'm still shopping around for an agent, but so far I haven't found one that fits my style."

Brian and I looked at each other.

"We should go inside," Brian said.

The front door of the mansion slid open automatically as we approached, and upon entering we found ourselves in a large open space where everything was bright white—the walls, the floor, and the thirty foot high ceiling. The only furniture was a single black chair in the middle of the room facing a ginormous rectangular video screen built into the wall.

"Not very feng shui," Stella said.

"What's feng shui?" I asked.

"It's an ancient Chinese method of arranging your furniture in a way that makes it harmonious with the natural surroundings," Brian explained. "This décor is more along the lines of wealthy modern sociopath."

In each corner of the room there were entrances to what appeared to be hallways. We looked around unsure of where to go next, but moments later Gor-Bot emerged from one of the hallways.

"Welcome to my son's home," Gor-Bot said. "Please follow me."

We followed Gor-Bot into the hallway he had emerged from, which looked like the one Brian and I found ourselves in after escaping Alien-Bot's jail cell. Every so often we would pass by a closed door or another hallway, but Gor-Bot just kept going straight ahead. It felt like we had walked ten miles before finally reaching a pair of closed doors at the end of the hallway.

"This is Sci-Bot's lab," Gor-Bot said.

The doors slid open and we followed him inside. I was expecting to see all kinds of high-tech equipment and test tubes and beakers and other science stuff, but instead we entered another huge white room that was mostly empty except for the dozens of video monitors built into the walls and touchpad control panels beneath them. Some of the monitors had live images of various places such as the airlock up on the atmosphere ceiling, the tube entrance, and the front yard of the mansion. Other monitors had long lines of code written in a language that didn't look like any language I had ever seen on Earth. This place looked more like a war room than a laboratory.

It took me a moment to notice that in one corner of the room there was a table with Sci-Bot on top of it lying on his back. His eyes were dim and his tentacles were hanging lifelessly off the sides of the table onto the floor. Once again a sharp fear shot through me that he was dead.

"Is he okay?" I asked worriedly.

"He is well," Gor-Bot said. "The repairs are now complete and have gone better than expected. This is because I have discovered something that has filled me with hope. During my thorough diagnostic scan of his cyborg systems, I discovered the remnants of some unusual code written in a language I have never seen before. This code was hidden

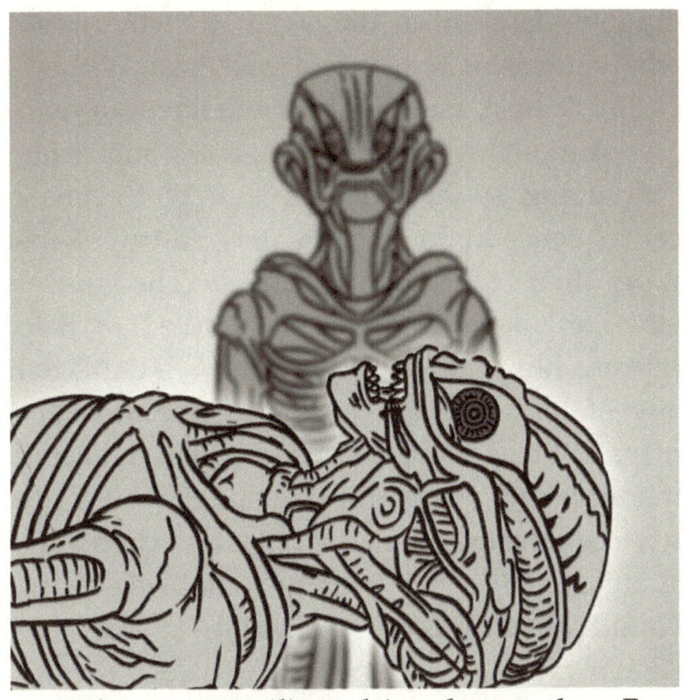

on a dormant auxiliary drive that modern Bots no longer use even though it is still part of our native hardware.

"I believe that this code was part of some crude virus he had been infected with. The reason we were not able to previously detect it is that our routine scans do not include this inactive auxiliary drive, which is constructed of relatively primitive technology and can hold only very small amounts of data. It appears that this drive was somehow activated and had been serving as a host for this virus, but the dragon's laser blast damaged it to the point where it was no longer a capable host. Without a capable host, the virus was unable to survive.

"Although we were trying not to injure my son, doing so has created a very fortunate consequence in that it ultimately destroyed the virus that caused his illness. The power etherizer likely would have worked to help capture him, but it would not have damaged any of his hardware, including the auxiliary drive. If I had run a routine scan that indicated there was no hardware damage, I would not have run the thorough scan that also checks the auxiliary drive, and it is very unlikely that I would have detected the virus—at least not right away, and perhaps for a very long time.

"As for the virus itself, I suspect that this is what created my son's artificial 'Alien-Bot' identity that had been suppressing his main 'Sci-Bot' identity and holding it prisoner. I thought I was going to have to call in the greatest psychological minds in the universe to figure out how to suppress or destroy the 'Alien-Bot' identity and free the 'Sci-Bot' one, but it appears that this has already happened. 'Sci-Bot' is now the only identity I am sensing, and there are no signs of the 'Alien-Bot' identity at all. You have freed my son, and

'Alien-Bot' is likely now gone forever."

"If Alien-Bot is gone, is Sci-Bot even going to know who we are?" I asked.

"I suspect that he will remember most of it," Gor-Bot said. "Even though his Sci-Bot identity was being suppressed, it still should have been forming memories. Perhaps it will seem to him like a bad dream. Then again, his brain is organic and has been through a great trauma, so it is possible that he may not remember any of it. Either way, we will soon find out. I was about to wake him just before you arrived."

"Do you think he's going to be mad at me for blasting him even though he's a good guy now?" I asked worriedly.

"I can see that you are still fearful of my son," Gor-Bot said. "I do understand that it may be difficult for you to face him after all that has happened, but he will most likely feel that he owes all of you an apology."

"But it wasn't his fault," Brian said. "He was sick."

"This is true," Gor-Bot said, "but my son is a good man with a strong sense of integrity and accountability, and though it was not his fault, he will still probably blame himself for allowing a crude virus to infect his mind, and he will feel that he should have noticed it before it took hold and that he should have been mentally strong enough to fight it off. I realize that this may not make sense to you, but I believe that apologizing will allow him to begin his emotional healing process, which is why I am asking you now as a favor to please stay and allow him to do this. I would certainly understand if you decide not to, and I am fully aware that you are anxious to return home to your families. But this would be very helpful to my son, as well as myself."

"I'll stay," I said. Brian and Stella also said they would stay.

"There is another thing I would like to ask for your help with," Gor-Bot said. "When my son and I were out exploring, we identified an uninhabited class M planet named 'Farglad'. This planet is in need of environmental repairs, as the previous inhabitants caused so much pollution that they unfortunately destroyed their living habitat and extinguished themselves. However, the solar system is very stable and should last for billions more years, and the planet has a small moon named 'Rainbow Rock' that has plenty of glacial ice on it that can be utilized for water.

"When we were attempting to help the

Kidokians, we suggested that they evacuate to Farglad and we would help them rebuild their civilization. Of course, the government refused and threatened us if we didn't leave. As I mentioned previously, we did eventually leave, but not before Sci-Bot sent the unencrypted open channel message to the entire population about how to create wormholes that would take them directly to Rainbow Rock. I now suspect that the response message that the government sent to Sci-Bot warning us never to return to their solar system also transmitted the virus that caused his illness. Such is the risk of sending a mass message over an unencrypted open channel.

"Anyway, Rainbow Rock is where I wish to go with my son. Hopefully he will agree to it. If so, we can begin work on repairing Farglad's environment and eventually establish it as the new home of the Alanian civilization. We will invite all Alanians who left here to join us if they wish. First, though, it would be helpful to use the *Universal Explorer* to transport our belongings and valuable artifacts to Rainbow Rock. After dropping us off, I am hoping you would be willing to take the *Universal Explorer* back to Earth and return it to Sven."

"Of course," Brian said. "He'll appreciate

that a lot."

Gor-Bot looked at his son and said, "It is time to wake him." He then put one of his hands on Sci-Bot's chest, and for a moment the elder Bot's eyes dimmed. It looked as if he was using his own energy to charge Sci-Bot, whose red eyes starting glowing brighter. When Sci-Bot's eyes were fully lit, Gor-Bot removed his hand from his son's chest. Sci-Bot then turned his head slightly towards his father.

"Father…" he said weakly. "How are you still alive?"

"I tricked you," Gor-Bot said. "You may be smarter than me, but I'm still a wily old Bot."

Sci-Bot then turned his head a little more so that we came into his field of vision. "The humans…"

"Do you remember all that has happened?" Gor-Bot asked.

Sci-Bot turned his head back towards his father. His eyes momentarily grew dim, and since the Bots don't have eyelids, I thought it was like their way of closing their eyes when trying to remember something. When his eyes brightened again he said, "Yes, I remember. I must apologize to these humans and the others." He then turned his head again to look at us. "Humans, please come closer."

I looked at Brian, but he was already looking at me to see what I was going to do. I then turned to Sci-Bot and looked into his eyes, and I could tell right away that I was looking not into the eyes of someone who wanted to destroy the universe but of someone seeking relief from the pain that he was feeling.

I stepped forward next to the table.

"This is Morgan," Gor-Bot said.

"I remember you," Sci-Bot said. "The green one. I saw you on Earth. You were being honored with the red one." Sci-Bot then turned his head a little more so he could see Brian.

"That is Brian," Gor-Bot said.

"To the two of you," Sci-Bot said, "I offer my sincerest apologies. I seem to have lost control of my mind and started behaving abhorrently. I became a... monster."

"You had a virus," I said. "But I can already tell that you're better now."

"The virus," Sci-Bot said. "The Kidokians."

"I believe this is so," Gor-Bot said. "I believe that the Kidokian government planted this virus to compromise your judgment and make you look incompetent so that their people would not believe your assessment that they were in danger. They saw you as a threat to their wealth and power. That was more important to them than the people they were supposedly governing."

"I wanted to save them," Sci-Bot said.

"As did I," Gor-Bot said. "As did I."

Sci-Bot then looked at Stella.

"What is your name?" he asked her.

"Stella Bella SuperStar from New York City," she said with a slight wave. "I hope you're feeling better."

"Yes, thank you," he said. "And I am truly sorry for what I have done. I hope you will accept my apology."

"Apology accepted," Stella said. "And thanks for giving me these cool powers!"

Gor-Bot then leaned closer to his son and said softly, "You now have a very important decision to make, and I am somewhat fearful of your answer. I need to know if you still desire to save Alania, or if you would be willing to rebuild our civilization elsewhere."

Sci-Bot's eyes grew dim for a moment.

"I wanted to save Alania," Sci-Bot said. "In a way I still do. But even when my mind was under the control of Alien-Bot, I realized that the effort was futile. I knew that even if I succeeded in saving our solar system, our civilization would never be the same as it was before. You cannot bring back the past, and why would you want to when it was far from perfect anyway?

"Father, you and I both know how sacred Alania is, but we must now allow nature to take its course. Even the sacred does not last forever, and there is no valid reason to continue allowing our native world to suffer any longer for the sake of our sentimentality. The most important part of a civilization is its people, and there are no longer any people here other than us."

"I am relieved to hear you say this," Gor-Bot said. "I had been concerned that you would still want to attempt saving our doomed solar system. Long ago I realized that it is sometimes necessary to let go of things you love regardless of how much it may hurt you to do so. Alania and Red-Gwot have been suffering for a long time, and it is now time to allow them to find peace. Therefore, we must let go of them and begin anew elsewhere. My suggestion is to go to Rainbow Rock, construct a lab, and begin repairs to Farglad for the purpose of building a new Alanian civilization. It is my sincere hope that you will find this plan agreeable, unless you have another idea in mind."

Sci-Bot's eyes once again dimmed

momentarily.

"I agree," Sci-Bot said. "It is sad to think of Rainbow Rock since it is the place where we hoped to save the Kidokians, but I realize that I must move past this sentiment. Let us gather our belongings and deactivate the life support mechanisms for Red-Gwot and Alania. Then we will proceed to Rainbow Rock."

CHAPTER 15

It didn't take long for Sci-Bot to regain enough strength to rise from the table and start walking around, a sight that at first still made me a little nervous considering how long we had known him as 'Alien-Bot'. But that went away after seeing Gor-Bot interact with him and how respectful he was to his father, and also because I no longer felt the presence of Alien-Bot anywhere in the room. It really did seem that the villain we had battled was now gone forever.

After Gor-Bot was convinced that his son was well enough to be left alone to pack for the move, he opened a portal to the cavern and the three of us followed him through it. On the other side, Gor-Bot stopped and looked around as if taking one last look at his old hideout.

"There are a few things I must gather from my lab," he eventually said. "I have actually been preparing for this moment for a very long time, as I always knew the day would come when I would have to leave this place for good. Fortunately that day has arrived under relatively peaceful circumstances. Although I have grown accustomed to the warm glow of these beautiful lava streams and falls, I look forward to once again being able to live openly beneath the light of a healthy star without fearing for my life every moment of the day."

In his lab, Gor-Bot quickly started packing various pieces of equipment into containers. The three of us joined in, and when a container became full, Brian and I would carry it onto the deck of the *Universal Explorer*. Gor-Bot left behind what looked to us like a lot of stuff, but he said it was nothing important and that he didn't want to bring an old mess to the new lab on Rainbow Rock. When everything was packed, we moved to the ship and helped Gor-Bot pack his personal belongings there.

It took about an hour before everything was neatly packed into containers. Afterwards Gor-Bot brought us down below deck to the control room, which he and Sven built into the bow many centuries ago. Since ships back then did not have wheelhouses or control rooms, it was really small and no more than two adult sized people could fit into it at the same time. And because of all the high tech equipment that they had squeezed into it, the room looked more like something from a spaceship than a Viking ship.

"This is where I taught my dear old friend Sven about space travel," Gor-Bot said. "In a way I have always felt bad about keeping his beloved ship for so long, but I was younger then and fascinated with this navigation vessel from Earth. We never had ships like this on Alania, even back when there were oceans here, because our ancestors were too afraid of the creatures lurking below the surface of the water. They almost always traveled by land or through tunnels dug beneath the oceans until they discovered how to create portals. At the time, though, Sven had become disillusioned with exploring the seas of Earth and was very eager to learn about space exploration. He insisted that he was fine with handing the ship over to me, especially since I would keep it safe from the thieves and rogues who were trying to steal it from him. He also said that he could always build a new one, but I do not believe he ever did."

Gor-Bot gave us a brief overview of the instruments in the control room, but he said we probably wouldn't have to worry about them because the ship had an automatic navigation system. All you had to do was tell it where you wanted to go and it would pretty much take care of the rest, including the opening of wormholes if the destination was far away.

Gor-Bot then said with the firm voice of a captain: "*U.E.* Command: Anchor up. Engines on. Shields at 100 percent."

Suddenly the engines started humming, and on one of the monitors we saw a purple laser shield surround the outside of the ship. Moments later the steamy lava air cooled and it felt like we had just stepped into an air-conditioned room on a hot summer day.

"That feels so nice!" Stella said.

"The ship is now entirely pressurized and climate controlled," Gor-Bot said. "We can now comfortably travel nearly anywhere in the universe."

"How fast can this thing go?" Brian asked.

"Not very," Sven laughed. "This ship navigates by opening wormholes and slowly 'sailing' through them, so to speak. Sven's old sail up on the mast is really just a solar energy collector used to fuel the low-power propulsion engine. Fortunately there's still enough energy stored on the auxiliary batteries to get us out of the cavern. While the laser shield protects the integrity of the vessel and provides a comfortable atmosphere for passengers and crew, the ship is still made of old Earth wood, so you have to take it slow."

"Well let's get going then!" Stella said. "I've been wearing this same outfit since leaving Earth and I don't want to be seen wearing the same thing two days in a row if it's already tomorrow back home. That would be a fashion faux pas if there ever was one!"

"Why don't you take the controls," Gor-Bot said to me. "Just say '*U.E.* Command' with a firm voice—the '*U.E.*' of course stands for '*Universal Explorer*'—and then tell it where you want to go."

"I don't know if I can," I said.

"Do you know how to speak?" Gor-Bot asked.

"Yes," I said, a bit annoyed at the question.

"Then you can do this," Gor-Bot said. "My son also used to fear things that he had never attempted, but he eventually got over it by realizing the value of experience. I always used to say to him, 'embrace what you do not know, and reject your fear of failure'. Even if you try something new and fail, the experience you gain from the attempt is still very valuable, and the failure itself something you can learn from. All the great scientists and inventors failed over and over again until they finally got it right. If you are really trying, you will eventually get better at it and start to build confidence. Confidence is built through experience, and it is far more powerful than any super power. Without it, you would not be able to do anything. So, go ahead and give it a try. No matter what happens, you will be that much more powerful for the effort."

I nervously stepped up to the control panel and looked around at the lights and gauges.

"Do not get distracted by all those fancy lights," Gor-Bot said. "Just tell it where you want to go."

"*U.E.* Command: Go to Sci-Bot's house," I said quietly—so quietly that I barely heard it myself. After a few seconds passed and nothing happened, I looked back at Gor-Bot.

"Say it with confidence," Gor-Bot said. "Let the ship know that you are the captain. Speak with authority. Do not be afraid."

I looked back at the control panel lights.

"*U.E.* Command: Go to Sci-Bot's house!" I said loudly, almost yelling, and the ship started rising slowly. Moments later a laser beam fired from the bow and opened a wormhole big enough for the ship to sail through.

"Well done," Gor-Bot said. "It is not necessary to shout, but you should always speak with confidence. Without confidence, your journey will be imperiled even before it begins."

Slowly and steadily we started moving forward towards the dark center of the wormhole. The calm orange glow of the cavern soon gave way to the erratic blue lightning that lined the wormhole walls. Moments later we exited Gor-Bot's secret hiding place for the last time.

CHAPTER 16

The *Universal Explorer* emerged at the other end of the wormhole high above the great blue lawn of the mansion, where Sci-Bot was already waiting in front of the main entrance with a large silver trunk resting beside him. The old ship slowly descended until we were hovering a couple of feet above the ground, and the engine continued to run even after the purple shield powered down.

"Is that all you are bringing?" Gor-Bot asked his son.

"Yes, Father," he said. "Most of what I need is already stored in my mind. I have brought some equipment and a few personal items, but I do not wish to convert Rainbow Rock and Farglad into 'New Alania'. Of course we will cherish and celebrate the old traditions of our culture, but we must also leave room for the new culture and traditions we will eventually establish at our new home."

Sci-Bot then stepped in front of the silver trunk, and behind him he used his four tentacles to lift it as if it weighed nothing.

"That's pretty handy," Brian said. "Maybe I should look into some tentacles for myself."

"Then how would you be able to fit into your desk at school?" I asked.

"Or sleep in your bed?" Stella asked.

"It would work if they were retractable," he said. "I'll have to talk to Sven it."

After Sci-Bot had boarded the ship, Gor-Bot told us that he wanted to be at the controls with his son so that they could navigate out of Alania one last time and get a good last look at the place.

"We are never going to see our home world again," he said.

"What's going to happen to it?" I asked.

"First we will deactivate the atmosphere shield around Alania," Gor-Bot said. "Then we will deactivate the outer container that holds the solar system together, as well as the tube that connects it to the main part of the universe. At that point there will be nothing left to hold the dark matter together. The solar system will eventually begin to tear itself apart, and any remaining clumps of matter will drift into the void. It will be interesting to see what happens with the leftover matter. Perhaps a clump of it will survive long enough to collide with another clump of discarded matter from the destruction of some other universe and spark a big bang that will create an entirely new one. I will be keeping an eye on that."

"Are there other universes already?" I asked.

"I believe so," Gor-Bot said. "I have never seen one directly, but from the unique vantage point Alania has at the very edge of our universe, I have seen a faint glow across the void that I am convinced are the light of others. This glow has always fascinated me, and ever since I was a child it has been a goal of mine to find out what it is."

"Are you sad that this is the last time you'll ever see Alania?" Stella asked.

"I feel more relieved than sad," Gor-Bot said. "Because our ancestors believed that our solar system was sacred, they did everything they could to keep it alive regardless of how much suffering their efforts caused Red-Gwot and Alania. Nothing in our universe is designed to last forever, not even the universe itself. This is why life itself is so precious."

"That reminds me," Brian said. "I have been working on a project for humans to achieve immortality. Although I can now see the flaw in that premise since the universe itself will not live forever, I still wouldn't mind living a few thousand or maybe even a million years longer than the normal human life expectancy. How long do Bots normally live?"

"Thousands of your Earth years," Gor-Bot said. "Sometimes tens of thousands, depending on how well you maintain yourself."

"Can we live that long if we had your technology?" I asked.

"I do not know," Gor-Bot said. "Every species reacts differently to the fusion of technology and organic life. Now that the three of you are human cyborgs, you are essentially the test subjects for your species. If your organic sides are agreeable to the technology, perhaps your species will begin a new stage of evolution. But that is only part of it. The key to living a long life is keeping your body, mind, and soul healthy."

After Gor-Bot and Sci-Bot disappeared into the control room, the ship's purple shield powered up and moments later we were climbing slowly towards the interior airlock doors of Alania's atmosphere shield. The three of us headed over to the starboard side and watched as the colorful splotches of melted houses and buildings down on the dark surface became smaller until they were tiny dots of color that eventually disappeared entirely. The blue dome in the distance soon flickered off like a neon sign in the night, and above us the red laser doors of the airlock silently slid open. After entering the airlock chamber, the interior doors slid closed below us, then above us the exterior doors slid open and the *Universal Explorer* calmly exited Alania's atmosphere for the last time. Since there was no longer any reason to close them again, the exterior doors remained open.

We started gaining speed as we got further away from the planet and eventually entered the tube that led us back to what was left of the Estarna Galaxy in the main part of the universe. Since Red-Gwot and Alania used to be part of Estarna, they were still relatively close and we had a good view of them.

The plan was for Gor-Bot and Sci-Bot to remotely deactivate the container surrounding the solar system and the tube connecting it to Estarna, then deactivate Alania's atmosphere shield. After deactivation, the ship would open a wormhole and proceed to Rainbow Rock.

There were other stars visible in Estarna, but they were dim and far apart. It was obvious that the galaxy was dying. From here the red laser container surrounding Red-Gwot and Alania looked like a deflating balloon that was barely attached to the rest of the universe.

We headed down below deck to see how the Bots were doing but did not disturb them. Their tentacles were hanging lifelessly down their backs, and Gor-Bot looked small and tired standing next to his big strong son. I felt sad

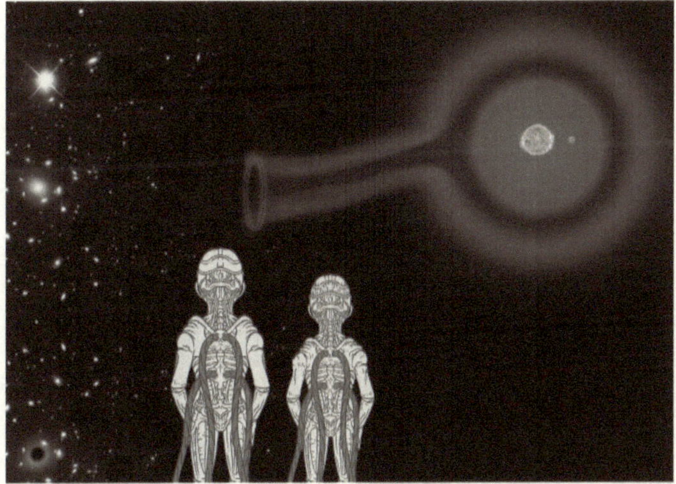

when the solar system container flickered and vanished, and even sadder when the shield around Alania suddenly disappeared. The release of the planet's atmosphere caused a barely visible shockwave that looked like the ripple on a pond after a stone had been thrown into it. Yet, even though the deactivation of these life support systems meant that Alania and Red-Gwot were going to die, seeing them without the artificial laser shields made them appear much more natural and beautiful.

"Our solar system looks so peaceful without the lasers," Sci-Bot said.

"Yes, it does," Gor-Bot said. "I have never seen it without those ugly red lasers, and I have never known a time in which our world was not dying. Our generations have known nothing but struggle to keep our beautiful solar system alive. These efforts have taken a tremendous toll on Alania, Red-Gwot, and our people. But now that long day is finally about to end, and soon a new one will begin. There will, of course, be new struggles, but it is a relief to be free of the struggles and suffering our world and our people have known for so long."

"Good-bye, old home," Sci-Bot said.

"Good-bye forever, Alania and Red-Gwot," Gor-Bot said.

The ship continued to sail slowly away from Red-Gwot and Alania, and soon the star was nothing more than a small red ball in the distance. Meanwhile, Brian, Stella, and I headed up to the food replicator on the main deck. I ordered a peanut butter and jelly sandwich, potato chips, pretzels, and a Zonka Cola. Brian ordered an entire pepperoni pizza and two Zonka Colas. Stella ordered a junior salad with no dressing and a lemon water.

"Is that all you're going to eat?" Brian asked Stella after she joined us at the table.

"Gotta watch the figure," she said disappointedly. She tried not to look at Brian's pizza, but she couldn't help doing so after each bite of her salad.

"The name 'Estarna' translated into English means 'first star'," Brian said, seemingly unaware that Stella was eyeing his pizza. "Estarna is even older than the oldest known galaxy our astronomers know about on Earth. But it doesn't have much time left. That is relative, of course. It may have a few million more years, but that isn't very long in a universal context—"

Suddenly a laser beam fired from the ship's bow and a wormhole appeared ahead of us. As the ship entered the wormhole, everything started turning blue from the glow of the lightning and it became difficult to hear each other because of the loud electric sounds.

Unlike the wormhole we passed through when leaving the cavern, it seemed like we were in this one for a very long time. I started feeling nervous that something was wrong, but the blue glow eventually disappeared and everything became calm again.

We were now in the Pirtea Galaxy, and it was easy to tell that we had arrived in an entirely different part of the universe, as the sky in every direction was filled with billions of brightly shining stars and galaxies. This part of the universe looked young and alive, much like our own Milky Way Galaxy. We got up from the table and headed back over to the starboard side of the ship and got our first look at the huge planet Farglad.

There were no clouds surrounding the planet, nor where there any patches of green. The land was brown and the oceans were such a dark shade of blue that they almost looked black. It almost looked like a dead version of Earth.

"I can see why Farglad is uninhabited," Brian said. "Even from up here it looks toxic. This is what I'm afraid Earth will look like someday if us humans don't change our ways."

The most amazing thing, though, was the sight of not one but *two* identical yellow dwarf suns that both looked like our own sun. Then, as if it been hiding offstage to make a dramatic appearance, the colorful cratered bands of Rainbow Rock slowly slid into view from behind Farglad. The moon was much smaller than the planet and looked much closer to it than our moon is to Earth, which made the sight even more spectacular.

"That is so awesome!" I said.

"I wish our moon looked like that," Stella said. "But I don't know if I could handle two suns. I would have to seriously upgrade my collection of sunglasses!"

As we drew closer to Rainbow Rock we noticed a blue light down on the surface. Upon zooming in we saw that it was a blue laser dome similar to the one that covered the empty city on Alania, only this one looked bigger and had more buildings under it.

"It looks like someone is already here," Brian said just as Gor-Bot was emerging from below deck.

"That appears to be the case," Gor-Bot said. "It has been several years since I checked in on this place, so I assumed that it would still be uninhabited. But since that time, someone came here and built a city down on the surface. We are not alone."

CHAPTER 17

Gor-Bot invited us into the control room, where Sci-Bot was looking at a monitor showing some of the buildings down on the surface. There was barely enough room for everyone, but we all managed to squeeze in.

"There appears to be a solar power grid and a water treatment plant," Sci-Bot said. "All of the buildings appear to be permanent structures. There are over a million people living here, but their identity signatures are encrypted with some unusual code that I have not yet been able to crack, so I cannot tell what species they are."

"That code," Gor-Bot said, then paused to point at a monitor that showed the program that was trying to crack the encryption. "That code is Kidokian."

Sci-Bot looked at his father.

"How do you know, Father?" Sci-Bot asked.

"It looks strikingly similar to the virus code that you were infected with," Gor-Bot said. "I realize that you have not yet had a chance to inspect that code yourself, but it looks very similar. Do you think the Kidokian government built this settlement?"

"No," Sci-Bot said. "If it had been the Kidokian government, they probably would have been threatening us or shooting at us by now. It has to be the Kidokian resistance. They must have found my instructions for opening the wormholes and coming here."

"How can you be so sure?" Gor-Bot asked.

"The government would not have risked losing their power by leaving Kidok," Sci-Bot said. "I followed the situation closely up until the end trying to figure out some way to save them before their star went supernova, which is what their own top scientists had been practically screaming was about to happen. The so-called leaders of this government vehemently rejected all the reports given to them by these scientists, then threatened them and their families for leaking this information to news reporters. They called these news reporters 'enemies of the people' and labeled their brand of journalism as 'fake news', even though they were the ones who were lying and endangering every single person on the planet. The reason they called us 'evil aliens' is because we had come to the same conclusion as their scientists. They eventually banned the free press for continuing to criticize them and spoke only to journalists who wrote favorable things about them. These favorable news outlets repeatedly attacked the credibility of the scientists and accused them of creating mass hysteria, but only the loyal government supporters who had been blinded by the promise of great prosperity believed any of this reporting. Government officials repeated these lies so often that they seemed to have brainwashed themselves into believing that they were in no danger and perceived any attempt at reporting the truth as an attack. They had imprisoned themselves and their supporters with these lies, and sadly it seems that they paid the ultimate price for it.

"Fortunately, it appears that those unwilling to follow the government over the ledge were able to organize, resist, and ultimately survive. It is sad to think that the government officials and their loyalists may have met an alternative fate, but this is the consequence of accepting what you wish to believe rather than the actual truth. I am sure that we will soon find out what happened to them for sure, and I hope they found a way to survive—but the Kidokian population was around two million, and there are only a little over a million here on Rainbow Rock now, so I do not expect the news to be good. As for the resistance, I am happy to see that they have apparently survived and so quickly settled into their new home. I feel that they will be happy here in this beautiful place, especially now that they are free of the lies and oppression they suffered for so long."

"They are hailing us," Gor-Bot said. "They are inviting us to land in the Great Park."

The ship descended towards a pair of large doors that started sliding open on top of the blue laser dome, and we were soon inside an airlock chamber just like the ones on Alania. A few minutes later we were under the dome, and down below we saw the large circular clearing of the Great Park in the exact middle of the city's brightly colored buildings. The surface of the park looked very much like the spiral pattern of a tie-dye shirt. The buildings immediately surrounding the park were the tallest in the city, while those beyond it became smaller in every direction all the way out to the houses at the edge of the city. Outside the city there were neatly sectioned rectangles of land that looked similar to what large farms on Earth looked like from above, but instead of being different shades of green, these farms included colors from all over the spectrum.

"Amazing," Gor-Bot said to himself. "It is truly remarkable what they have built here in such a short period of time."

"The Great Park looks like a tie-dye version of Central Park!" Stella said. "I love this place! I wouldn't mind living in one of those buildings down there overlooking the park!"

"This place is so cool!" I said. "It sure does make West Plains look boring!"

Closer to the surface we spotted small dots moving around the park that began to form a cluster. In the middle of this cluster the dots left a circular clearing where the tie-dye surface was still visible.

"Are those the Kidokians?" Brian asked.

"Yes," Sci-Bot said. "They have made a clearing where they want us to land."

Only yesterday it would have been impossible to imagine the being we had originally known as Alien-Bot becoming emotional. Yet, here was the physically identical Sci-Bot with an expression on his face of one who had not seen a beloved friend or family member in a very long time. He then started making a low moaning noise, and as he did so the bright red glow of his eyes became dim.

"I think he's crying," Brian's telepathic voice said in my mind.

Gor-Bot also began making a similar noise, but moments later these noises became higher pitched and their eyes started glowing brightly again. Then their eyes started changing colors, the red gradually changing to orange, then yellow, then green, and all the way around the spectrum until they became red again. This was one of the coolest things I had ever seen and I wanted to ask if they could make my cyborg eye do that, but I didn't want to disturb them.

"Tears of joy," Brian's voice said.

The *Universal Explorer* soon stopped descending and settled into a steady hover a couple of feet off the ground. The purple laser shield surrounding the ship then made a zapping sound and disappeared, and the five of us left the control room and climbed up to the starboard side of the main deck.

There before us extending out in every direction was a sea of Kidokians, a species of hovering beings whose bodies were of all different shapes and brightly glowing colors. The shapes of their heads matched the shapes of their bodies, so some of them had square heads and square bodies, some had triangle heads and triangle bodies, and some had

shapes so unusual that I couldn't even name them. In the middle of their heads they each had a large single eye with a mouth below it that was just a straight line. Their arms were shaped like large hot dogs, but they had no hands or fingers. Instead of legs, each had a trapezoid-shaped thing that was glowing on the bottom and must have been what was allowing them to hover. They all had strange symbols on their chests, but it was hard to tell what these could have meant because the people who had identical symbols weren't standing near one another. But the strangest thing may have been that their different body parts didn't appear to be physically attached and looked as if they were being held in place by magnetism or some other invisible force.

Another strange thing was how quiet they were. There was no crowd noise or any sign that they were talking to one another. But when we leaned over the rail of the ship and they got their first look at us, they all raised their arms above their heads and started waving them while making bubble-popping noises with their mouths.

"What are they doing?" Stella asked.

"I think they're cheering," Brian said.

"This is remarkable," Gor-Bot said. "They

were pale and sickly the last time we saw them. They did not have any glow."

"They were an oppressed people," Sci-Bot said. "Their leaders called them the opposition for merely expressing fear that their world was in danger."

"That doesn't make any sense," I said. "They were trying to save everyone."

"Great power can corrupt the mind," Sci-Bot said. "The Kidokian government was apparently more worried about losing their power than they were about their world being destroyed. Systems of unbalanced wealth and power are a threat to any civilization, including yours on Earth. Yet, it is reassuring to know that there are people like the Kidokians who are willing to fight back against a government that serves only the interests of some while oppressing the rest."

Gor-Bot turned to face the three of us.

"Thank you, my friends, for helping my son and I get to this point where we could witness such an incredible sight," he said. "After so much struggle, we, like the Kidokians, have finally found peace. But now it is time for you to finally return to your own homes and families. All you need to do is tell this ship where to go, and then enjoy the ride."

CHAPTER 18

It turned out that the surviving Kidokians managed to escape to Rainbow Rock not long before their star went supernova. The entire solar system was destroyed and a massive black hole was left in its place. More than half of the entire Kidokian population was saved thanks to the resistance effort, the turning point of which was when activist hackers intercepted Sci-Bot's open channel message before the government had a chance to delete it. The message included instructions on how to open local wormholes that would take them directly to the surface of Rainbow Rock and how to build a laser biodome there that would protect them from the elements.

Since the Kidokian government did not

have surveillance systems in place that could detect open wormholes, the resistance was able to open them in discreet locations all over the planet without being detected. They organized a massive escape plan and instructed citizens to pack their essential belongings and as much food as they could, and to be ready to leave the moment they received a message that would include directions to the nearest designated wormhole location. Otherwise, they should go about their lives as usual and not discuss these plans with anyone because the government would surely try to stop them and send them to prison, or worse.

The message was sent during the night of a major government holiday that marked the tenth anniversary of "The New Constitution" being signed, a document that the new populist government hastily wrote when they initially took power. Their first act in office had been to immediately repeal the original Constitution that had been in place for thousands of years and replace it with this new one. In honor of this "great achievement", just about the entire population of Kidok was given the day off so that everyone could participate in the many rallies and celebrations that had been scheduled, although no one expected the "whining and complaining" non-supporters to show up. The government supporters didn't want them there anyway with their "stupid protest signs and annoying chanting", so they boasted victory when not one single protester showed up at any of the events.

As darkness fell and the celebrations kicked into overdrive, families from all over the planet quietly started emerging from their homes and traveling to the nearest wormhole with all the belongings they could carry. Teams of organizers were also transporting food, equipment, and supplies through other wormholes that would help them build their new society on Rainbow Rock. Cheers from the nearby government rallies could be heard in the background, but none of the revelers noticed the mass evacuation that was taking place in the shadows behind them.

After a long night of partying, government officials woke up the next morning all groggy and disoriented to the shocking discovery that more than half of the Kidokian population had disappeared. They also discovered a message sent to them by organizers of the resistance explaining what had happened, and that all the wormholes had been left open for anyone who wished to join them on Rainbow Rock. All remaining residents, as well as government officials and their family members, would be welcomed and their safety would be guaranteed. The message also warned that any hostile action taken against the settlers on Rainbow Rock would be met with a fierce defensive response.

The resistance had also sent out a similar message to the remaining population on Kidok inviting them to Rainbow Rock. However, government officials quickly got wind of this and scrambled to send out a message of their own announcing that the traitorous opposition party and their cowardly supporters had fled and were now suffering on the cold barren surface of a tiny moon millions of light years away with little food or chance of survival. These alarmist dissenters would no longer be able to spread fear and hysteria with fake news stories reported by dishonest reporters who were attempting to delegitimize a government that was merely trying to bring back prosperity to the Kidokian people.

"A wonderful new day has arrived on Kidok," the message said. More celebrations and rallies were immediately planned all over the planet. The government and its supporters would now finally be able to build paradise their own way without the opposition party trying to stop them at every turn with their "ridiculous rules and regulations".

The message also went on to reassure the remaining citizens that they were in no danger whatsoever, and that their star was more stable than it had ever been in its entire history: *"Bigly stable, more stable than any other star in the history of the universe… it is disgusting that these traitors spoke so poorly of their own star! SAD!"* Additionally, government officials were working hard to build walls around the "dangerous wormholes" that left the "real Kidokians" exposed to all sorts of "dangerous alien criminals and bad dudes" from the outside world who could just walk right in and wreak havoc on their society. To protect their citizens from these dangerous aliens, the government would be posting armed guards at each wormhole while the walls were being built. However, the message didn't mention that the guards were there not only to make sure that none of the "bad dudes" got in, they were also under strict orders to make sure that none of the remaining Kidokians got out.

The message also didn't say anything about the chaos that was happening behind the scenes at the Kidokian capital. Many government officials who knew that their bosses were lying about the star were now secretly planning to escape through the wormholes. A few who acted quickly enough managed to make it, but most were caught and immediately arrested along with their families.

Meanwhile, hardly any of the citizens who had supported the government even tried to leave. They rejoiced that the opposition was gone and continued to eat up the lies being fed to them by their beloved leaders who came to power under the promise that they were going to destroy the establishment and rebuild their society back to the greatness it once knew. They truly believed that they would finally get the better lives they had been promised, and that those who had been preventing that from happening were now gone for good.

After a week of celebrations but little evidence that promises made to their supporters were being fulfilled, the government continued to assure the public that everything was running smoothly like a finely tuned machine. More rallies were scheduled, and government officials continued to promise that more jobs and higher wages were on the way, and that the highest standard of living in the history of Kidok was on the horizon.

But at the government level, reality finally started to take hold when their star began showing obvious signs of instability. Coronal mass ejections became frequent and kept knocking out the main power grid, and while the government continued to reassure the public that everything was fine, behind the scenes there was panic, chaos, and infighting. Some knew that they were in trouble and urged the others to work together on a plan to quickly evacuate the population to Rainbow Rock, but these voices were quickly shut down by those who continued to argue that the coronal ejections were normal and would eventually settle down. The important thing to them was to make sure the public continued to believe everything was fine so that they wouldn't start to panic.

The government didn't want anyone to start thinking about fleeing to Rainbow Rock, so their news service continued to publish stories about how the "cowardly dissenters" who fled were suffering terribly in their new home. Of course, these stories were total lies, yet government supporters believed them even though not one single person who fled to Rainbow Rock had attempted to return.

The government supporters had no way of

knowing that things were actually going very well on Rainbow Rock. The biodome had been built and temporary shelter was set up prior to the migration, so the new arrivals were quite comfortable and were able to get right to work building permanent infrastructure, housing, and farms. There was plenty of work to do, and everyone was willing to do their part. A new government had also been formed that was based on the original Kidokian Constitution that had worked brilliantly for thousands of years before the current regime took over and started changing all the rules to give themselves more power.

Then the bad news came. It had finally happened. Kidok's star went supernova and destroyed the entire solar system, leaving behind a black hole that is now essentially a cemetery in space. Gone were any signs that the planet of Kidok or its inhabitants were ever even there.

On Rainbow Rock a monument was built and dedicated to the memory of those who had been lost on Kidok, but it also served as a reminder that the truth should never be compromised. There was also a monument built in the memory of Gor-Bot and Sci-Bot, who were believed to be dead because the

Kidokian government news service had reported that their ship was destroyed shortly after Sci-Bot had sent the instructions for opening wormholes and building the biodome. Obviously this was a lie, but the surviving Kidokians were not sure because they never heard from them again and were unaware of Sci-Bot's illness.

So it was a cause for great celebration when the *Universal Explorer* arrived on Rainbow Rock with Gor-Bot and Sci-Bot alive and well and planning to stay. Even though Rainbow Rock was originally considered by Gor-Bot and Sci-Bot as a temporary home while they repaired Farglad, the Kidokians liked the tiny moon and wanted to remain there permanently. So, Gor-Bot and Sci-Bot said they would help the Kidokians on Rainbow Rock and also begin repairing Farglad as a future home for Alanians or any other refugees who had fled their homes due to natural disasters, war, oppression, government corruption, or any other reason.

Gor-Bot also showed the virus code that had infected Sci-Bot to one of the Kidokian hackers who helped organize the resistance. The hacker was able to confirm that it was indeed created and planted in Sci-Bot by the

Kidokian government and had ultimately helped spawn the 'Alien-Bot' identity that went on to threaten the existence of the universe. The hacker said it was not unusual for the government to hack and plant viruses in the technology of their political enemies, but to hack a living being for the purpose of defending a lie that ultimately led to the death of a million people was incomprehensibly evil.

While it was an incredible story that had a happy ending for the Kidokians on Rainbow Rock, it was still disturbing to think that there were those out there like the Kidokian government officials who were willing to allow their own people to suffer for the purpose of accumulating even more wealth and power than they already had, which was already far more than they needed.

"Unfortunately, our own people on Earth haven't learned this lesson yet," Brian said. "Hopefully we can share this story with them as a warning, but there are going to be plenty of people who won't believe us and will even attack us for it."

"What can we do then?" Stella asked.

"Resist," Brian said. "We just have to keep fighting for the truth and calling out the liars. Eventually, even those who are loyal to the liars may eventually realize that they are being used. The liars aren't interested in helping them, they are only interested in accumulating more wealth and power. Hopefully a catastrophe won't occur before the loyalists finally realize that they are being played like a video game."

It was sad to say good-bye to Gor-Bot and Sci-Bot, but at least we knew that they had found a new home. Sci-Bot again apologized to us and said that we can contact him if we ever needed help on Earth. He then looked at me.

"You are a true hero, HyperKid," he said. "The humans of Earth are fortunate to have you looking out for their best interests."

"Thanks," I said. "I'm sorry if I hurt you with the laser blast."

"The blast cured me," he said. "For that I will be eternally grateful."

CHAPTER 19

I felt both happy and sad as the *Universal Explorer* slowly rose above the surface of Rainbow Rock. The Kidokians were all applauding, and standing tall above them in the crowd were Gor-Bot and Sci-Bot waving at us with their arms and tentacles.

As we approached the airlock on the biodome ceiling, the ship's purple laser shield zapped on and the huge striped sail ascended up the mast. Shortly after passing through the airlock, a laser beam fired from the bow and a large wormhole opened in front of us.

The plan was to drop Stella off first, then take the ship back to West Plains and return it to Sven. After passing through the wormhole we emerged into the bright blue skies above

New York City, where the autumn rays of the late afternoon sun gave the buildings below a golden tint.

"There's Central Park!" Stella said. "Woo-hoo, I'm home! Over there! We need to go to the north end of the park near 110th Street!"

We descended towards a grassy field on the Fifth Avenue side of the park where a few people were throwing a football around. They stopped and looked at us for a moment, then resumed throwing the ball like it was no big deal to see a thousand year old flying Viking ship land in Central Park. Even more amazing

was that nobody else nearby even looked in our direction and kept on doing what they were doing like it was just another day in the park.

"Typical New Yorkers!" Stella laughed. "It's good to be home!"

"Do you live close to here?" I asked.

"I wish!" Stella laughed. "There used to be some affordable places to live up at this end of the park, but not anymore! I live up near Sugar Hill about forty blocks from here. But no worries, I know the subways like the back of my hand. Oh, wait, I forgot I can fly now!"

I too had forgotten about our flying abilities because I didn't think we would have them on Earth, but Stella just pointed her hand in the air and took off.

"Chirp me on InstaChattaSpaceBook!" she called to us as she soared towards the skies above Manhattan. No one near us even noticed her, not even the people throwing the football.

The ship's engine started humming again and we were soon slowly rising above Central Park. After clearing the skyline, we had an amazing view of Manhattan all the way down to the Freedom Tower and the Statue of Liberty out on the water. Such a sight made me feel like a super hero in this great city that has had so many of them, including Coney Island's own Hot Dog Guy.

The ship then turned north and headed towards the suburbs. About twenty minutes later we started descending towards the baseball field at West Plains Elementary, and to our surprise there was a huge crowd waiting for us below.

"Typical West Plainers," Brian said.

The crowd was cheering loudly, and there was a huge video screen at one end of the field that showed the exact view that I was seeing as if I was holding the video camera myself.

"That's strange," I said to Brian. "Do you think they've been watching us the whole time on that video screen?"

"We saw everything!" Sven's voice said

through the intercom in the control room. "My baby is finally home! I've already decided to rename her the *U.E. Gor-Bot*. Welcome home, boys!"

After the ship landed and we put the boarding ramp out, the next thing I remember was that my feet were finally back on Earth and I was in a tight family hug with Mommy, Daddy, and Parker. A few feet away Brian's mother was hugging him, and Sven was standing just beyond them. Then I caught a glimpse of the big video screen and again noticed that it was showing the same exact view that I had, which made me wonder if I had a camera attached to me.

"Could you really see us the whole time?" I asked.

"Yes, we saw everything!" Mommy said. "We even saw you guys on Alania. I was so worried! I couldn't look when you were flying towards that dragon, but you were amazing!"

"We're so proud of you, son!" Daddy said, holding up his hand for a high five.

"But how could you see us?" I asked. "We were billions of light years away!"

"Ha!" Sven said and took a step closer. "I actually set up a video feed for your parents through your transformation scanner and made a tiny mobile wormhole that the feed could travel through all the way back to Earth. They were able to see what you were seeing in real time, and they were nice enough to share the feed on the big video screen here so that everyone in town could watch. But don't worry, they turned it off when you were using the bathroom. In fact, your father played some commercials he made for selling HyperKid t-shirts during the breaks. Anyway, you can disable the camera now yourself if you wish."

"But why did the message I sent to my parents say it was going to take 45 billion years to get there?" I asked.

"I didn't think to connect the messaging system to the scanner, so it didn't go through the wormhole," Sven said. "Sorry about that."

"That's okay," I said. "At least they were able to see what has happening."

"Listen, Morgan," Mommy said, suddenly turning serious. "While we are very proud of you saving the universe, I really wish you had eaten some green beans or some other vegetable with those pancakes. And I really wish you wouldn't have drank all that Zonka Cola. Do you have any idea what that stuff will do to your teeth?"

"Can we go home and play video games

now?" Parker interrupted.

Daddy, meanwhile, was staring at the eye of the octopus on the back of the ship and seemed to be in a trance just like when he was staring at the painting in Sven's office.

"Ship…" he said out loud to himself.

"It's good to be home," I said.

CHAPTER 20

I thought that saving the universe would earn me at least one day off from school, but noooooooooo, not with my parents.

But I'm actually glad I went to school the next day because Mr. Cooldude threw a big party in honor of Brian and I. The theme of the party was Hawaiian luau, and the classroom was decorated with fake palm trees, tiki figures, and palm grass wrapped around all the desks. After snacking on pineapple chunks and drinking sweet coconut milk from plastic coconut cups, Mr. Cooldude had us push all the desks to the side of the room so that the ukulele player and luau dancers could perform for us. Then some caterers came in and set up a buffet of traditional luau food, including poi, kalua pig, lomi-lomi salmon, and squid. None of the kids wanted anything to do with this food except for Brian, so he and Mr. Cooldude feasted while I ate the peanut butter and jelly sandwich that Mommy packed in my lunch.

The smell of the food spreading through the hallways was apparently too much for Mrs. Crabcake to resist. She eventually wandered in and Mr. Cooldude invited her to help herself. Now that she was no longer on her bean diet, she sampled everything at the buffet except for the squid and then came back for seconds and thirds.

After lunch Mr. Cooldude said it was time to honor the heroes who saved the universe. The other kids clapped and cheered for Brian and I, and Mr. Cooldude played a highlights video of our adventure that had already gone viral on ViewCube. Everyone cheered again when it was over, then Mr. Cooldude asked us to come up front to tell everyone about the experience in our own words.

I always got really nervous whenever I had to speak in front of the class, but Brian seemed fine with it and started talking. Unfortunately, he skipped over all the interesting parts and instead talked about technical stuff like the physics of wormholes and the heat and light properties of laser blasters. When Mr. Cooldude saw that Brian had lost the crowd, he interrupted by thanking him and asking me what I was most proud of.

I thought about it for a moment.

"I'm proud that we saved the universe," I said. "I'm also proud that I was able to help Sci-Bot. He really is a good person and a great scientist. We all thought he was a bad guy when we didn't know his side of the story. It kind of reminds me of last year when we thought Brian was a bad guy at first. I guess you just need to get to know someone and understand their situation before you know if they're a good guy or a bad guy."

"Well said, Morgan dude," Mr. Cooldude said and started clapping. The other kids started clapping too until Gina let out an eardrum-piercing scream that caused everyone to cover their ears.

"What's the matter, Gina?" Mr. Cooldude asked worriedly.

She screamed again and pointed towards the window. At first I didn't see what she was pointing at, but I did hear some weird grunting noises. Then I saw a patch of grass start to move and what looked like a pale disfigured hand poke through from underneath. Then on another patch of grass I saw the head of what appeared to be a zombie with glowing eyes sticking out of the ground. The zombie was attempting to wriggle itself up out of the ground to the surface, and as it was doing so it suddenly shot a pair of laser beams from its eyes that blasted a hole in the ground.

Gina screamed again while the rest of us said, "Whoa…"

Soon the entire field had zombie hands and heads sticking out of the ground. The ones that had managed to climb all the way out were now wandering aimlessly and erratically firing laser beams from their eyes and making a big mess of the playground.

"I think I know some of those dudes," Mr. Cooldude said.

Meanwhile, Brian was over at the buffet

fixing himself another plate of squid and poi. He was the only person in the room not looking out the window. I went over to him and tried not to look at or smell the squid on his plate.

"Don't you see the zombies out there?" I asked him quietly so that the other kids wouldn't hear.

"Sure," he said. "But first I'd like to have some more of this squid. It tends to get a little rubbery if it sits out too long."

"Hey," Gina called to us. "Aren't you *so-called super heroes* going to do something about those laser zombies out there?"

Brian and I looked out the window and saw one of the female zombies fire laser beams from her eyes towards a woman holding some grocery bags on the other side of the playground fence. Fortunately the beams missed the woman, but they blasted a big hole in the fence and caused her to drop her groceries and run away screaming.

"This situation is quickly becoming pretty gnarly, dudes," Mr. Cooldude said to us.

The work of a super hero is never done, which is why I now understand what it means in comic books when they refer to "the super hero's burden". Daddy sometimes refers to "the writer's burden", which he explained was how writers often feel obligated to include every single little detail to tell the full story. He also explained how it is sometimes difficult to figure out where to end a story because some of them just go on and on and on—but that's where the beauty of sequels kicks in.

That's why this is probably the best place to stop this story and give it a happy ending before the laser zombies have a chance to ruin it. Besides, Daddy is very tired right now and is about to fall asleep at the keyboard. This book has turned out to be much longer than the last one, and he's having trouble keeping up with all of my adventures. He says it's important to work hard and to do as much as you can, but you also have to realize what your limits are or else you're going to have a nervous breakdown. I guess I understand that. I know that it's impossible to save the day every time, but I hope everyone else will understand this when something happens and I'm not able to help.

"Don't worry about being a hero," Daddy told me. "While it feels good when people praise you for your heroic actions, at the same time they're also raising their expectations of you to levels that are impossible to meet. But their expectations should not be your concern. Just do as much as you can with the understanding that if you try to be the hero for every single thing that happens in the world or even just in West Plains, you'll wind up in the super hero cuckoo house like Green Bean Man when he tried to make every kid in the world eat vegetables.

"Just be yourself and don't let others define you. If you can accept who you are and not worry about what everyone else wants you to be, you'll be fine."

ABOUT THE AUTHORS AND THE BOOK

Emerson Daub is a fifth grader who has a healthy interest in cyborgs, super heroes, and video games. His father Richard is a writer and former journalist who likes to watch baseball, eat cheeseburgers, and listen to old guy rock & roll music.

While sitting down to write with pen and paper or in front of a keyboard isn't exactly Emerson's favorite activity, he has a wonderful imagination and loves to make up characters and stories. So, once again he and his father have combined their talents to produce *The Cyborg at the End of the Universe*, the second book in *The Adventures of HyperKid* series (the first of which is titled *HyperKid v BullBorg*), and the third book overall they have written together (the other being an illustrated children's book titled *Spaulding and Zoom* about their family's pet cats).

Over a period of two weeks during the summer of 2016, the father-and-son writing team set aside some time each day to hash out the story. Emerson began where the first *HyperKid* book ended with Alien-Bot wanting to destroy the universe and how it would be up to HyperKid and BullBorg to stop him. When Richard asked why Alien-Bot wanted to destroy the universe, Emerson explained that Alien-Bot believed that the rest of the universe was responsible for destroying his beloved home planet of Alania, which at one time was the home of a great civilization of Bots but had now fallen on hard times, and that the only way to save it was to destroy the rest of the universe and use its resources to restore it to its former greatness.

Emerson also wanted to include a new super hero in the book and came up with the idea of a beautiful, charismatic girl from New York City named Stella Bella SuperStar. This new character continues the theme that began with the first *HyperKid* book, that those who are different in superficial ways may have more meaningful things in common, and that in order to save the world it will be absolutely necessary for people from all walks of life to work together to fight the real enemies of bullying, intolerance, and prejudice that are the root causes of so many major problems in contemporary global society.

THE BOOK THAT STARTED IT ALL...

HyperKid v BullBorg is the highly acclaimed HyperKid origin story that has inspired kids and adults all over the world. Go back and meet Morgan Wallace for the first time when his dream of becoming a cyborg super hero comes true and he is challenged right away by Brian Bullini, a.k.a. BullBorg. At first Morgan thinks Brian is his arch enemy, but the two eventually learn that they have more in common than they initially realize, and together they are able to rise above their personal obstacles to defeat the real enemies of bullying, intolerance, and prejudice. The story includes a humorous cast of characters that parodies the world of super heroes and the growing pains often experienced by fourth graders, as well as the growing pains parents and teachers experience in raising and teaching them.